BANKING HER

A BILLIONAIRE

NOVELLA

max monroe

Banking Her (Billionaire Bad Boys, #2.5)
Published by Max Monroe LLC © 2016, Max Monroe

ISBN-13: 978-1537292137
ISBN-10: 1537292137

Editing by Silently Correcting Your Grammar
Proofing by Indie Solutions by Murphy Rae
Formatting by Champagne Formats
Cover Design by Perfect Pear Creative

DEDICATION

To Dedications.
No one ever dedicates their dedication to the Dedication, but it
does such an awesome job of being dedicated. So here's to you!
But, um, you should probably do a better job in, like, bars and at
weddings and stuff. You're always so sloppy and drunk and shit.

Oh, and to cake. You're delicious.

CHAPTER 1

Wes

Light reflected off the glass of her office window as I approached the end of the hall. It was late and I was tired, but if she was going to leave lights on all over the goddamn place, some compulsive part of me wouldn't let me leave without turning them off.

Taking leisurely strides, I pulled out my master key from my pocket and rounded the corner, only to pull up short when the interior of her office became visible through the slats in her blinds.

Long, tan legs crossed at the ankles and up on the edge of her desk, Winnie Winslow sat staring at the file in her lap, a pen twisting and turning between the plush pads of her pink lips. Her normally perfectly placed blond hair was a wreck, as though she'd been running her hands through it, and the crisp edges of her white blouse lay untucked at the top of her skirt.

It was a natural progression for me, following the line of her temptingly exposed skin in an explorational effort to find more, but as a line formed between her dark eyebrows, my gaze shot to her face.

She was concentrating on something, but I couldn't decipher the nuances of it enough to know if she was confused or frustrated or both. It was startlingly clear to me, however, that I wanted to be able to tell the difference.

The thought made me scowl.

Goddammit. The last thing I needed was some unavoidable siren's call at work—from some woman who drove me absolutely insane by just sitting there doing her job.

The longer I stood, scanning the muscles of her legs as they rubbed together restlessly and watching her breath puff through her lips in little pants, the angrier I got.

Watching her as she studied something else felt too good, like I could get my fill without her judging eyes and harsh looks urging me to hurry it along and get down to business—on her terms.

It was a compulsion, and every time I thought I'd gotten enough to satisfy the craving, she'd shift or twist and a new inch of skin would expose itself at the top of her thighs or on the inside swells of her fucking incredible breasts. Five minutes of unabashed attention later, with steam making a bid to shoot right out of my nose, realization dawned.

Fucking hell. This was, by far and large, the *creepiest* thing I'd ever done. I couldn't find it in me to proclaim Winnie Winslow innocent in many ways, but she was right now. Harmlessly staying late at a job where she didn't get paid overtime, staring into the files of players and cases and timelines and God knew what else for the greater good of *my* team, and I was out here watching her like a fucking psychopath.

Resolute in my newfound self-loathing, I quietly turned back from her office toward the direction I'd come. But I only made it two steps before karma saw fit to torture me for my behavior with the bleating, annoying ring of my cell phone.

"Shit! *Fuck!*" I cursed as I juggled the folders in my hands and shoved a hand into my pocket to retrieve the offending electronic device. It was a test of willpower so mighty I thought I might bust out of my suit, shredding it to pieces, and turn right into the Hulk. But I must have had some latent superpowers because I didn't turn around to look into the window of her office again.

When the name of my ill-timed caller flashed across the screen, it took all I had to answer normally—without f-bombing all over the goddamn place about how inconvenient it was to be friends with him.

"What?" I asked as I put the phone to my ear, tucking the nearly scattered papers under my arm for safekeeping.

"You talk about the way I answer the phone, but you answer it like a fucking prick. Every time," Thatch said.

"Yeah, well, I'm busy. And last time you called it was because you were trying to con me into doing one of Cassie's late-night craving runs for you."

He laughed, the fucking bastard.

"I only do the work for pregnancies I create, and I had not one moment of fun or involvement in the creation of that little hellion."

Though, truthfully, I had *heard* the sound of their fun plenty of times. The horny little exhibitionists couldn't seem to keep their clothes on, no matter where they were or how many people were listening.

"Wes?" I heard from behind me, Winnie's sweet, self-assured voice making me squeeze my eyes together. Of course, she couldn't just let the fact that she'd seen me out here go.

"Oh, hey, Winnie," I greeted. "I didn't realize you were still here."

Liar.

"Look out, Winnie," I heard my most annoying friend say directly in my ear. "Pinocchio's nose is only seconds away from poking you right in the pussy."

I fought the urge to curse Thatch out, laugh, and, hell, maybe even cry. I was normally stoic, so much so that I'd earned a public reputation for it, but it seemed like I couldn't control my reactions anymore. So breaking down in tears might not have been that far off.

"You need me to look at something?" I asked Winnie.

Thatch pretended to cough in my ear before murmuring, "Her pussy."

She shook her head and then nodded, seemingly undecided, and the glimpse of uncertainty had my eyebrows pulling together of their own accord. In my relatively short time around Winnie Winslow, she didn't do uncertainty. She was one hundred percent confident in all of her decisions and remarks, and I'd come to expect that from her.

I opened my mouth to speak again, when she straightened, her long legs getting longer, and any curve befalling her spine disappeared.

"Only if you want to. I was just looking over the MRI results from Mitchell's hamstring injury."

It'd been a couple of weeks since Mitchell's initial reinjury, and we were expecting him to play this weekend. I couldn't really afford to not have him play. She didn't say anything had changed, but maybe looking at the MRI myself wasn't a bad idea.

"Okay. I'd love to see the MRI. Just give me a second to finish up this phone call, and I'll be in."

She nodded and swung her body back into her office with the help of her hand clenched around the doorjamb. My gaze followed her as she strutted to her desk and rifled through the papers, pulling something out from the bottom of the stack. She started to tuck her shirt back into her skirt, and I jerked my eyes away when she looked up self-consciously in my direction.

"Well, well, well. Late nights with Ms. Winslow. Someone's a naughty boy."

Something didn't add up with Winnie—the whole interaction reeked of not-quite-right—but thanks to Thatch in my ear, I couldn't seem to figure out what.

My attention back on Thatch, I spoke into the phone in an angry whisper. "I didn't even know she was still here, asshole. Jesus."

His laughter rang out through the phone loudly enough that I had to pull it slightly away from my ear.

"Me thinketh my fair Whitney doth protesteth too mucho."

I shook my head and rubbed at my temple, keeping the folder clenched tightly with the pinch of my elbow. "That doesn't even make sense."

"Come on. The sooner the two of you bang, the sooner we can all go on a tropical vacation together. It'll be like that movie, *Couple's Retreat.*"

"Don't like seventy-five percent of the couples in that movie break up?"

"Okay, so it won't be like *Couple's Retreat.* It'll be like a totally better, porno version of it. No one breaks up in porn."

"Of course, no one breaks up in porn," I told him, following him down the rabbit hole of conversation without even realizing it. Thatch was the master of dragging you into insanity without your knowledge. I think it was the matter-of-fact way he talked about absurdities. "It's an explicitly no-boundaries situation."

"It's an accidental anal situation."

"Exactly. In real life, women break up with you for accidental anal."

His voice turned grave. "Is that why there's so much tension with Winnie? I thought it was because you hadn't fucked, but it's because you gave her accidental anal, isn't it?"

"Jesus Christ! No." My whisper turned harsh as I took a couple of steps away from Winnie's office and checked to make sure she couldn't hear me.

"It's not accidental anal. There's no anal."

"Oh. So that's the problem. I've gotta tell you, Wes. Even I haven't gotten anal. And if I can't get anal from Cassie, you're never getting anal from Winnie."

"I don't want anal from Winnie!"

Thatch laughed, and I closed my eyes in frustration. "So just the pussy, then?"

"I'm done talking to you."

"Wait!" he called before I could hang up. "I called for a reason."

"I'm not going to get ice cream for Cassie."

"That's not—"

"I know nothing about pregnancy panties."

He barked laughter. "Well, you know more than me. I wasn't aware there were pregnancy panties—"

"I don't have access to any fried pickles, and I absolutely will not bring you Chinese food."

"You know, I'm really starting to question your opinion of me, Whitney."

"That's fine," I told him. "I've been questioning my opinion of you forever, in that I have one to give, because I'm still friends with you despite the fact that you are one of the most ridiculous human beings I've ever met."

"It's the big dick."

"What?" My voice was incredulous and completely fucking confused about how we'd gotten here.

"Why you're friends with me. The big dick."

I laughed then. "No, no. I can assure you my friendship has nothing to do with, and I quote, 'the big dick.'"

"Come on. You know you wouldn't want to be friends with some little-dicked guy."

"I'm pretty sure I want to be friends with the guy who doesn't tell me about his dick size."

"Huh." He managed to sound like *I'd* surprised *him.* "Well, you're out of luck there."

"Thatch, I'm hanging up now."

"Wait!"

God help me. I glanced over my shoulder once more, but in my attempt to do it inconspicuously, I completely failed to see anything. Apparently, subterfuge wasn't my specialty.

"I just want to know what safety precautions you have on board your plane."

My eyebrows shot together. "What?"

His voice turned suddenly serious. "I know Cassie has that shoot coming up for your away game—"

That wasn't for a couple of weeks. Did I really have to deal with this now? "Thatch—"

"And I'm really trying not to get in her face about all the traveling and everything because, yeah, she'll pretty much cut my big dick off, but I just need to know."

I still didn't even understand what he was asking. "I'm not following here."

"What kind of medical provisions do you have on the plane?"

I glanced back into the office at Winnie, and actually caught sight of her this time, to find her sitting behind her desk and staring at the ground. I wondered if she was trying to avoid looking at me as hard as I was trying to avoid looking at her.

"Well, Winnie will be on the plane with us. And she's a doctor."

"Yeah, yeah, okay. That's right." He exhaled, and for the first time in this entire conversation, I didn't want to wring his motherfucking neck.

I was a lot of things, a fair many of them probably not good, but I could tell when something genuinely meant something to him. "She'll be fine," I told him gently.

"I know. Fuck. I just can't stop myself from worrying."

I shut my eyes. Goddamn this big fucking sap. When he was vulnerable like this, I could barely even stand it. He was so damn *genuine*. "That means you're going to be a good dad."

He didn't say anything, and I felt my chest tighten.

"I promise that Winnie will look out for her," I told him. I knew he needed the extra encouragement, and in that moment, I wanted nothing more than to give it to him. "She's more than capable, and you know that, no matter what, I'd make sure Cassie got the help she needed."

"I know."

"Thatch—"

"I'll let you go," he interrupted. "Go do anal with the good doctor."

The line was dead before I could respond.

I shook my head to clear it and then turned to walk into Winnie's office. I didn't bother knocking as I walked through the already open door.

"Thatch?" she asked, and I raised my eyebrows.

"How could you tell?"

She put a finger to the skin between her own eyebrows and explained. "You always get a line, right here, when you talk to him."

I laughed and shook my head, and then, for some reason, shared. "He's really nervous about Cassie's pregnancy. I think he calls me and Kline because he's afraid to smother her about it."

She looked me right in the eye, and for the first time in as long as we'd been working together, I didn't feel the hot lash of her anger burning through me.

CHAPTER 2

Winnie

"Well, he's not the only one nervous about her pregnancy," I added for some insane reason. I was thrown off by this entire interaction with Wes. Our history of conversations was short but definitely had an undertone of aggravation or annoyance. I often found myself wondering if he could even stand being in the same room as me. Hell, I had a hard time being stuck in close quarters with *him*.

Sure, physically, Wes was the absolute perfect picture of my dream man—tall, fit, and Lord Almighty, his hazel eyes whispered promises of hot, mind-blowing sex.

But then, he'd open his mouth and pretty much ruin *everything*.

He needed a muzzle.

And to stop questioning every single one of my decisions related to the Mavericks. I honestly thought he made it a point to challenge me. It was like he obtained some sort of enjoyment out of being the one person who consistently disagreed with me.

Which made it completely ridiculous that I had asked him to come into my office to look at Mitchell's MRI. I was the physician between the two of us. Not him. Sure, he was the owner, the one who signed my checks, but he had zero medical background; therefore, his opinion didn't mean jack shit.

Yeah, but you didn't ask him into your office for intellectual conversation. You want to ogle his fine ass in that suit...

I did. I *really* did. And I was torn between thinking I was a genius for luring him into my office so I could stare at his ass, versus realizing I had reached an all-time low. The truth of it was, I hadn't even been looking at Mitchell's MRI—it just seemed like a good excuse to get him inside. But hell, it had been over a year since I'd last had sex, and Wes Lancaster had a really fantastic ass.

Yes, you heard that right.
One whole year.
Three hundred and sixty-five days.
Five hundred twenty-five thousand and six hundred minutes.
But who's counting, right?
Obviously, me. I'm counting. And it's a wonder my vagina hasn't packed her bags and fucked off to somewhere else where single-mom responsibilities and work hours aren't a priority.

The last time I had sex was a drunken night of regret with Lexi's father. Nick had been in town for Lexi's preschool graduation, and I'd caved on letting him spend the night at my house. And I'd justified it by telling myself I was merely letting our daughter have more time with her father before he left again for who even knew how long.

It wasn't that Nick was a shitty father, he was just an absent father.

Needless to say, after our daughter had gone to bed, we'd

shared a bottle of wine, and then another, and then another, until my brain had only been able to focus on how much I missed the feel of a man. In me, around me, I had just needed to be kissed, touched, *fucked*. I'd needed to feel like I was desirable again. I had needed an orgasm that didn't occur from my own devices.

In that moment, with Nick, my ex-boyfriend from a relationship that ended in an unplanned pregnancy and a disastrous breakup, I'd just needed sex.

And that's all it was. Sex, pure and simple.

It was an epically stupid choice, obviously.

Now that a full year had passed since that wine-fueled decision, my brain was starting to feel the effects, frequently fantasizing about what it would be like to have the kind of sex that made your hands fist the sheets and sweat trickle down your skin. The kind of sex that left you wanting more. The kind of sex that made sleepless nights worth the fatigue.

God, I want that kind of sex. I want it so bad.

"Not the only one?"

Wes's voice pulled me from my sex-fogged thoughts, and I stared back at him in confusion.

Not the only one? What in the hell was that supposed to mean? He wanted to have sex, too? Right now? With me? "Huh?" I asked eloquently.

Could I have sex with Wes? No-strings-attached sex?

Naked. Rough. My hands clenching his hair. His hands clutching my ass as he thrusts inside of me. His lips to my ear, whispering dirty things that have my nipples tightening from the sheer audacity of his filthy mouth...

Welp, no need to phone a friend, there's your answer.

He tilted his head to the side, and a slight smirk crept across his full lips. "You said Thatch wasn't the only one nervous about Cassie's pregnancy."

"Oh…oh, right." My cheeks heated in embarrassment. Sweet baby kittens, I had been three seconds away from ripping my blouse off and mounting him on my desk. I cleared my throat and rubbed my now sweaty palms down the top of my skirt. Shit, I was losing it, sitting here, fantasizing over visuals of Wes spreading me out over my desk and burying his face…

For the love of God, I needed a shrink.

Or an orgasm…from Wes Lancaster.

I pushed those thoughts aside and grabbed my phone from the top of my desk and unlocked the screen, my fingers quickly finding the group text conversation with Cassie and Georgia. I held it up for him to see. "Georgia has been demon-texting me and Cass for the past seventy-two hours. She's not too happy Cassie is traveling so much."

He took the phone from my hand and started to read a few of the texts aloud. "Goddammit, Winnie Winslow. You're a doctor. Help me out here! Tell Cassie she's not allowed to travel anymore. It's not healthy for her or the baby." His hazel eyes shone with amusement, and he glanced up at me with a grin. "How far along is Cassie again?"

"Three months. You'd think she's forty weeks and ready to deliver with the way Georgia is trying to put the kibosh on all of her travel plans. She's hell-bent on Cassie being put on bed rest for the rest of her pregnancy."

"Wait…forty weeks? I thought it was nine months?"

"Ten months, actually. Due dates are calculated at forty weeks."

"Damn," he groaned while a small smile kissed his lips. "It's about to be a long seven months for all of us."

I laughed. "Yeah. It definitely is."

My phone pinged with a notification as Wes continued to read the insane text messages Georgia had been sending Cassie and me. His brow furrowed, and he quickly averted his gaze from my phone. "Here," he said, handing my phone back. His voice no longer tinged by warmth and amusement. Instead, his tone hinted at irritation. "You got a text message."

"Oh, thanks," I said, but I couldn't help the confusion wrapped around my words.

What the hell? That was the quickest one-eighty I had ever witnessed in my life.

This man was a conundrum of surly mood changes and rare smiles. Well, at least around me, he was. I had noticed when his friends were around, his smiles were more frequent, and he never held back his witty retorts and sarcastic quips. But around me, and the public, he seemed less thrilled, less laid-back, and more jaw-clenchingly vexed.

I couldn't shake the feeling of wishing Wes would give me more of his smiles, his laughter, that easygoing charm I knew lay beneath his broody layers.

It was stupid, I knew that much, but I couldn't stop myself from feeling that way about him.

My phone pinged and lit up with three more text notifications, and I finally glanced down at the screen to find the group chat with my four older brothers flooding with their mindless chitchat, that generally revolved around razzing each other and asking me to do favors.

Remy: When's Mom's birthday?
Jude: The same day. Every fucking year, Rem.
Ty: I hope Winnie buys her something nice and lets us sign the card again.
Remy: Seriously. What day, you fucks????
Flynn: Winnie, how much do we owe you for Mom's gift?
Jude: Yeah, Win. How much? If it's over two hundred, I need to borrow money.

Ty: Says the idiot who just sold his "vacation home" in the Hamptons to buy a bigger "vacation home" on Martha's Vineyard.
Flynn: How Jude can walk the fine line of cheap and pretentious is mind-blowing.
Remy: WHAT DAY IS MOM'S BIRTHDAY???

See what I mean?
I chuckled and typed out a response.

Me: The 28th and get your own fucking gift for Mom.

"So?" Wes's voice pulled my attention away from my phone. "Are we going to look at Mitchell's MRI, or are you going to keep texting with *Remy?*"

My brow furrowed at the way he said my brother's name—until my brain caught up with his insinuation. He thought Remy was a date or a boyfriend or basically anything but a blood relation.

I opened my mouth to offer a rebuttal of, "Um, Remy is my brother," but quickly thought better of it and stopped myself.

It wasn't any of his goddamn business.

And why in the hell did he sound so pissed about it?

Whatever. *Maybe this is what I need to hold him at arm's length since I'm so obviously failing at doing that on my own.*

I set my phone on my desk and handed Mitchell's MRI report to him. "I think he should be good to play by Phoenix."

He quietly read the report and then looked up to meet my eyes. "You don't think he can play the game against Minnesota this weekend?"

"No." I shook my head and focused on what I knew would be a fight. I hadn't planned this discussion, really, but it was obviously one we needed to have and one I knew wouldn't go easily. "I think he should sit out one more week and continue to go through physical therapy sessions twice a day."

"This report is telling me otherwise, Dr. Winslow."

Go figure, I was *Doctor* now. It seemed Wes referred to me as Dr. Winslow when his stodgy, pissed-off persona came to visit. Basically, it was the equivalent of my mother using my full name, Winnie Marie, when I was a kid and in a shitload of trouble.

"Yeah, well, that report is just that, a report," I retorted hotly. Unfortunately for everyone, the bad in him seemed to bring out the antagonism in me. "I'm looking at the full scope, the big picture, and I'm assuming you want Mitchell healthy and playing for the duration of the season, and hopefully, the postseason."

"That goes without saying."

"Well, it goes without saying that I want that too," I reminded him. "Which is why I'm not clearing him to play until Phoenix."

"You're not clearing him?" He held up the MRI report. "After reading this report, that decision seems a bit conservative, don't you think?"

I shook my head and crossed my arms over my chest. "No. I don't think it's conservative at all. I think it's the right decision."

A humorless laugh left his lips. "Why even ask me to look over the report if you were already set in your final decision?"

"Ultimately, it's your team. I just figured you'd like to know."

And I wanted you to come into my office so I could ogle the way you fill out your pants. *Son of a bitch.*

"That's right, it is *my* team," he repeated with far too much venom. "And I'll be honest, Mitchell sitting out in Minnesota doesn't sit well with me."

"It doesn't sit well with me either."

He tilted his head and scrutinized my expression. "Are you sure? Because from here, it doesn't seem like you're having too difficult a time digesting the news."

I stepped closer to him, meeting his eyes without flinching or backing down. "I actually got this report two days ago. I've been mulling over this decision for the last forty-eight hours."

"Interesting." He stepped closer, and his voice dropped a few octaves when we were practically nose-to-nose. "And you didn't think to ask me to discuss this forty-eight hours ago?"

"No," I whispered angrily. "I didn't need your assistance, *Mr. Lancaster*."

"Well, *Dr. Winslow*, next time, you let me know the second these kinds of reports come in."

"Fine," I snapped.

"Fine."

Neither of us moved, our faces mere inches from one another. It was a world-record-worthy stare down, and the longer we held it, the heavier the air seemed to become. My breaths came out in exaggerated waves, my chest practically heaving up and down and brushing up against the buttons of his dress shirt.

I wanted to smack him. I wanted to swallow him whole.

He blinked. I blinked.

My cell phone vibrated with a call against my desk, but it didn't even register on my radar.

His eyes searched mine until they flickered down to my lips, to my heaving chest, and then back up to my lips again.

I wanted to crush my mouth to his so I didn't have to listen to his fucking questions.

I wanted him to kiss me.

His mouth moved infinitesimally closer. My mouth followed suit.

He was close, so close now I could feel the warmth of his breath brush across my lips. One more inch and our mouths would be touching. One more inch and we'd be sharing the same air. One more inch and I'd know what Wes tasted like against my tongue.

One more inch…

The obnoxious ring of my desk phone broke our ridiculous trance, jolting us into action—and away from each other. Concerned it might be Lexi's babysitter, I walked around my desk on shaky legs and picked up the receiver. "Dr. Winslow."

"Winnie," Georgia's voice filled my ear. "Why aren't you answering your phone? And why are you at work so late?"

"Because I'm busy working, Georgia." I sighed and stared out the floor-to-ceiling window of my office. I couldn't decide if it was the best-timed phone call or the absolute worst.

"Can I call you back—"

"No!" she shouted into my ear. "This is an emergency, Win!"

"It is not an emergency." Cassie's annoyed voice joined the line.

"Go ahead and take the call, Winnie," Wes interrupted. My eyes met his and we searched one another's gaze for something, but I wasn't sure what. Desire? Want? Need? *Regret?*

His eyes flickered down to the hand clutching at the silky material covering my chest, and I abruptly let go, feeling like an idiot for being so affected by him. The green notes of his hazel eyes flared brighter as he briefly looked at my lips again, but any depth of warmth disappeared as his gaze met my own. "I've got to head out anyway."

"Who is that?" Georgia questioned.

"Is that Wes?" Cassie chimed in. "Are you in your office with Wes?"

"I'll call Mitchell on my way home," he added.

"Holy shit! That's definitely Wes!" Georgia's voice shrieked, and I had to pull the receiver away from my ear before my eardrum started to bleed.

"Are you playing naughty secretary and naked boss tonight, Win?" Cassie singsonged.

"She's a physician, Cass. Not a goddamn secretary."

"I know, Wheorgie. It's called role-playing."

Even without the help of speakerphone, their voices echoed inside my office. I quickly tapped the hold button before they started saying things I'd prefer Wes not to hear.

"You're going to call Mitchell?" I asked, curious what exactly he was going to tell him.

He nodded. "I'll let him know we've decided that he won't be ready to play in Minnesota, but if he follows your orders and physical therapy schedule, he should be good to go by Phoenix."

My eyes widened in surprise. "We've decided?"

"Yes," he agreed. "We've decided."

My brow furrowed in exasperation. Partly because of our ongoing battle, and partly because I couldn't read him like I so desperately wanted.

Obviously, he knew my decision was the right decision, but why in the hell did he always have to find an argument with everything?

Before I could respond, my office phone started ringing again. Those impatient bitches had obviously hung up and called back on a different line.

"I think you better get that." He chuckled lightly and headed for the door, but he turned back to look me in the eye before he left. "Have a good night, Winnie." He sounded surprisingly sincere.

"You too."

With one last nod, Wes was gone, and Georgia's rambling filled my ear again. "Don't ever put me on hold again, Winnie Winslow. Not when we've got an emergency. And anyway, why was Wes in your office so late?"

I plopped down in the leather chair behind my desk and slipped off my heels, resting my tired feet on top of my desk. "I was showing him Mitchell's MRI results, Miss Nosy.

"Were you also showing him your puss-ay?" Cassie asked.

"Of course. Who do you think handed him the MRI report?"

Cassie laughed. "You have a flair for bedside manner, Dr. Winslow."

"Are you leaving the office now?" Georgia asked.

"Probably in about five minutes. Why?"

"You need to stop by Cassie's apartment on your way home."

Cassie groaned.

"Why?"

"Do you have latex gloves and some lube handy?"

"*What?*"

"She needs her cervix checked. She's been crampy, and I think she might be going into labor soon."

"I'm three months pregnant, Wheorgie. And I'm pretty sure it's the chili-loaded nachos I had for dinner that are making me cramp."

"You don't know that!"

"Fine," Cassie retorted. "I'll have Thatch's cock check my cervix before I call it a night."

"Count me in, honey!" Thatch's voice boomed in the background.

"See? Problem solved, G."

"No! No! Problem not solved! That could make it worse. Sperm can induce labor!"

"I really wish you'd stop reading pregnancy books."

"Georgia," I chimed in. "Cassie isn't going into labor, and even if she were, there is no way in hell I'm going to check her cervix."

"But you're a doctor, Win!"

"Yeah, but I'm not an obstetrician, sweetheart. Unless she thinks she sprained her vagina, I'm zero help in the pregnancy department."

"I'm coming to get you, Cass. We need to go to the emergency room."

"Oh, for fuck's sake. Would you just take a breath? You sound crazier than me, and I'm pregnant and my baseline level of crazy is higher than most."

"Are you bleeding, Cassie?" I asked, trying to steer this conversation into less outrageous waters.

"Nope."

"Leaking fluid?"

"Nope."

"Do you still have cramps?"

"Nope."

"See, Georgia? Cass is fine. Her baby is fine. Everything is fine. You have nothing to worry about."

I really hated to admit when Wes was right about anything, but he had hit the nail on the head with the whole "this is going to be a long seven months" sentiment.

"Okay. Okay," Georgia finally voiced. "I just don't want anything to happen to you or my godson, Cass. I worry, okay? And you're just traveling so much. It's freaking me out a little."

"Godson?" I asked.

"She's convinced I'm having a boy," Cass explained. "And let's get back to the whole Wes being in your office after hours thing. Now *that* is something I want to hear more about."

I groaned. "It wasn't like that. Just because your vagina's need to bone all day, every day, is strong enough it could serve as a backup generator for the entire city, doesn't mean we're all sex-crazed."

"But I didn't say anything about sex," Cassie teased. "I think the real question here is why are you thinking about sex?"

"I'm hanging up now."

"Denial is the first sign you have a problem!" Georgia's voice was the last thing I heard before I hung up the phone.

They were right. I had a problem, all right. I was pretty sure I'd almost kissed Wes Lancaster in my office, and I was also pretty sure the regret I felt had nothing to do with the situation, and everything to do with the interruption.

CHAPTER 3

Thatch

"What was that I heard about needing to check your cervix with my Supercock?" I asked Cassie as she hung up the phone. Arm extended, I handed her the glass of ice water I'd just prepared and watched the line of her throat as she chugged it.

She'd been so fucking thirsty since we found out she was pregnant—both for actual liquid and for sex. So much so that she'd been making a bid to kill me by dehydration—sperm dehydration, to be technical about it.

"He's got a medical background," I went on inanely, filling the silence as she drank. "It was more as a medic in the Army than as an actual, honest to goodness doctor. So he hasn't seen much pussy in the medical sense, but he's definitely familiarized himself with a cervix or two outside of business hours."

She narrowed her eyes, and I laughed, surrendering with both hands raised.

"Hey, I'm just giving you his resume. I'm only a messenger sent here to help you decide whether or not you think he'd be a good fit for your cervical dilation monitoring needs. I, personally, think he fits the bill perfectly."

Finally done with her water, she reached forward and set the glass on the coffee table with a laugh. "Will you stop fucking babbling?"

I shook my head and pulled her bare foot into my lap, putting the pressure of my thumb right into her instep. "Look at who you're talking to."

"Jesus fucking Christmas," she pretended to grumble around a groan of foot-massage ecstasy. "I guess I'm going to have to let your Supercock fly into my tunnel to get you to stop talking, aren't I?"

I smiled and tilted my head back and forth briefly. "Well, I don't know that it'll make me stop talking so much as it will turn everything I say exponentially dirtier."

A full-body shiver ran from her toes to her nose, but she did her best to hide it.

This was one of her new games, pretending to be put out by the idea of chasing several orgasms in a row—a kind of role-playing, if you will—and I had to admit, I found it endlessly fascinating.

Other men might have been offended, but the way she did it was in such obvious disagreement with the desires of her body, it'd be pointless to take it personally.

Instead, I played her game, talking her into it in all the creative ways I could think up, and she rewarded me by coming twice as hard.

I'd also do just about anything to keep her happy during her pregnancy. All the books suggested happiness could do nothing but help in the quest for healthiness, and keeping her and my little girl safe was my biggest priority.

Okay, so I am speculating that it's a little girl, but I figure the universe, knowing what it knows about me, will be out for blood.

And torture. And making me spend twenty-to-life in some maximum security prison when she becomes of age for little hormone-ridden boy-men to chase her all the goddamn time, shooting their sperm out of their tiny penis guns, and doing their damnedest to make my head explode.

About twenty minutes after Cassie had thrown the positive pregnancy test at my head, my whole world had changed. Not in the obvious sense or the way I behaved, but in the way my mind prioritized tasks for the day. Number one had been forever and irreparably changed to *Keep Cassie and our baby safe.*

It wasn't a conscious choice. It was an absolute. A rule that not only wouldn't but *couldn't* be broken.

"Earth to Thatcher," Cassie called, waving a hand in front of my face. Internally, I cringed at the fact I'd taken a nice little detour into Worryville again. Unfortunately, I'd become a frequent visitor, unable to deviate from the track that led me there. Somehow, though, I'd managed to mask my worry with something else in front of Cassie. I wasn't sure exactly how it came across—probably as stupidity—but she seemed comfortable with whatever front I managed to put on.

"I know I acted like I didn't want to bone, but that's our thing. I cry wolf about not wanting any pussy pleasure, and you steamroll me all the way into the bedroom, tongue my pussy for a few minutes, and then get down to business. You're supposed to have your dick in me by now, for fuck's sake."

As always, she brought me right out of my head and into the room—onto the very couch where she sat, where I could smell the citrus on her skin. She was too goddamn entertaining for any moment spent with her to be unpleasant. I laughed. "I don't know, honey. Is that how it feels to you? Because your rundown isn't making me feel like I'm doing a good job of being memorable."

Her snap was like the lash of a whip. "What the fuck are you talking about?"

I tried not to smile bigger, but it was a real fucking challenge.

"I tongue your pussy for a few minutes?" I asked, and then bit my lip when fire flamed in her eyes. "Is that really the best description you can come up with for it?"

"I'm trying to hurry through this talking bullshit—"

I ignored her, reaching for her across the couch, picking her up with two hands on her ass and settling her on my lap, straddling me, her perfect pussy cradled directly on my already hard dick.

"If that's what you think," I told her quietly. "I'm going to have to teach you a lesson."

Her nipples hardened right before my eyes.

Goddamn, I love her tits.

"Ooh," she cooed. "Sexy professor and naughty student?"

I shook my head with a smile and then nipped at the skin below her ear, the roar of blood in my own ears drowning out the background noise of the TV.

"Private tutor and—" she started, but I pushed my lips to hers before she could finish.

"No, baby," I said softly. "This one is all Thatch and Cassie."

She squeaked as I rose to my feet, keeping my hands at her ass and her up with me. She clung to my shoulders and shoved her tits toward me in invitation.

An invitation there was not one fucking single inkling of a chance I would deny.

"Get rid of the shirt," I ordered, and she didn't delay. Up and over her head, she pulled it off, confident in my ability to hold her in my arms.

My lips closed around the pink of her nipple as soon as the soft cotton of her T-shirt cleared it.

As her head fell back and her hands clamped tight around my

neck, I moved one of my hands to the middle of her back for extra support.

Cassie hardly ever had inhibitions, but when we came together like this, what few she had vanished instantaneously. Moaning and gasping, she tried to get her body closer to mine, to climb right inside me, and her tits were leading the way.

Jesus, when she pushed herself farther into my mouth like that, it was a struggle not to fucking eat her alive.

"Oh, God," she groaned, rubbing herself against me as I quickened my step. The sounds of her pleasure were like a telegraph to my dick: *Things are speeding up. We need you, General. Get here and provide internal support as quickly as possible.*

Her back hit the bed softly as a mewl of protest escaped her lips. I hadn't followed her down, instead standing tall to pull my shirt over my head and shove my shorts and boxer briefs to the ground. She didn't have much clothing left—a tiny pair of boy short underwear the only thing she'd put on her bottom half after her earlier shower.

I caught sight of her packed bag in the corner as I dropped to my knees. The bag indicated that I was down to just hours before she left again for work. But I put that out of my mind and concentrated on pulling Cassie's boy shorts down with my teeth.

She pushed up onto her elbows on the bed and watched me as I did.

"Are you going to tongue my pussy?" she teased, and the lilt of her provocation lit up my world. No one made me happier than she did, and punishing her for her smartass remarks with a silent drag of my tongue would never ever get old.

I did just that, trailing it up from ass to clit and watching her eyes roll back in her head. Her long eyelashes seemed to sparkle as she fluttered and squeezed, alternating between the two reactions because what she was feeling was too overwhelming for just one.

"Son of a motherfluffing monkey biscuit," she gritted out through a moan, and I laughed.

I'd been teasing her about cleaning up her language, something she obviously had plenty of time to do given gestation time and then the delay in our baby's ability to cogitate. Even if our daughter was a little baby genius, which she was obviously likely to be, we were looking at a solid eighteen months. Still, Cassie had taken it at least a little to heart—she still cursed up a storm, but there was effort there—and it made me want her more.

It was these little hidden morsels of her that no one else saw or understood that augmented my love to the point of madness. She was so much more than most people knew, and many of her secrets were only for me. When she was selfish now, it wasn't just for herself—it was for her, me, and the little peanut-sized baby we'd created.

I closed my eyes and breathed her in. Her spunk, her smell, her goddamn unbelievably addictive taste...all of it overwhelmed me as I licked her, alternating between fucking her pussy with my tongue and flicking at the sensitive bud above it in varying rhythms. She writhed, but I held her legs open with a clench of my fingertips on her thighs.

You're not going anywhere, honey.

"Thatch," she cried out urgently, but I knew she wasn't coming yet.

This was another one of her games, one that made me smile into her pussy and lick her harder. She was close to orgasm, so close that she started to feel like my tongue wasn't enough, like she needed my dick more than the air she needed to breathe. But still eager for at least a little control, she didn't want to ask me for it. She wanted me to be the one who gave in, the one who couldn't take any more, and she'd learned if she pretended she was there, I might think she was too.

It was complicated and deliberate, but it was also completely subconscious. Her mind was powerful when she knew what she wanted, so much so that she could convince her body to play the part no matter how much it might argue.

"Good try, honey," I told her on a ragged whisper. "You come on my tongue first, and you do it right fucking now."

The muscles in her thighs tensed, turning to sexy, sweaty rock under my fingertips as she finally gave in to my command and all the evidence of her excitement flooded my mouth in a rush. I sucked it up, lapping and drinking until I couldn't take it anymore—until I nearly came into empty air.

Pushing her knees to her chest, I climbed up from the floor and over top of her, entering her smoothly with one sure stroke.

She cried out, and I damn near just cried.

I'd never felt anything better than being inside of her, skin on skin, all that wet, loving warmth. If I'd known how good it would be, I probably would have tried to get her pregnant earlier—like, the first night we were together.

She moved her hips to meet mine, and as much as I tried, I just couldn't help myself. "The report is in, honey," I told her, my voice jolting with each stroke. "Your cervix is in tip-top shape."

"Shut. Up."

I laughed and leaned down to touch my mouth to hers. She licked and nipped at it, and I got off on the fact that she loved the taste of herself on my lips so much.

"Come on, baby," I taunted, trying to push her there faster, desperate for her to come because my orgasm was coming up my spine like a goddamn NASCAR driver.

"Oh yeah, oh yeah, oh…yes!" she chanted as she finally let go. I shot my load immediately.

Her gaze followed me as I took her in—messy hair, soft, sexy eyes, and nearly bruised lips. Her tits were out and peaked and so fucking inviting, I buried my face right in the middle of them.

Fuck me, she is so fucking hot.

She laughed, and the rumble from her chest made me tingle all over.

"I love you," I told her. She pulled my face from her tits and looked me right in the eye.

"Okay, fine. Supercock can be my cervix's personal doctor."

My wink rang out like a shot in the air, and her answering smile nearly knocked me on my ass. "That's Dr. Supercock to you now. After that many years of schooling, he wants you to use the title."

CHAPTER 4

Cassie

The stark contrast of black ink and Thatch's tan skin glowed in the barely there moonlight. Obviously a little sliver of white showing in the dark night sky rather than the bright circle of a full moon, it illuminated our room just enough that I could make out all of the planes, ridges, and valleys of muscle on my man.

He slept while I thought, an endless loop of unavoidable realities trickling through my mind.

Over the next six months, I'd be traveling all over the place, filling up my schedule with enough photo shoots to supply a year's time. It was insane, but it was a means to an end. A way to fulfill all of my obligations and still have the freedom to take a minimum of four months off for maternity leave, six months if I was lucky.

Finances weren't my motivation for the crazy work schedule. I was fortunate that money wasn't an issue for me or my future child. My soon-to-be husband had more money than he knew what to do with, and my photography career had padded my savings nicely, even allowing for a hefty chunk of cash to be invested.

When I found out I was pregnant, my first thought had been, *"Holy shit, that idiot knocked me up!"* followed by a pregnancy test bouncing off of Thatch's big head. My second thought, having occurred when he fell to his knees and pressed his lips to my belly, was *"I love him and his Supercock for giving me the greatest gift I've ever been given."* And the third thought had occurred a few days later, during a photo shoot for one of the most elusively picky magazines in the country: *"I want to be able to have both, a family and my career."*

It was that third thought that had driven me to reschedule the photo shoots I would end up missing when I went on maternity leave. It would have been easier to let them go, not to worry about missed opportunities or what-ifs, but when I really thought about it, I knew I didn't want to lose what I had worked so hard to achieve.

But now, lying in our bed, with Thatch sound asleep beside me, I was wondering if this ridiculous work schedule was the right choice. I'd already been traveling more, knowing I needed to front-load the extra work as much as possible, because the bigger I got, the harder everything became. But the more time I spent away from Thatch, the more I hated being away from him.

Hated. It.

Lonely nights spent in hotels without his big body wrapped around me like a second skin while his head utilized my boobs as pillows were getting old real quick. He was my rock, the one person I could trust with everything. The man who could fuck me senseless and pleasure my puss-ay in ways I never knew were possible. The man who let me get all kinds of filthy in the bedroom—but never failed to treat me like a fucking princess.

It was hard being away—for days on end—from that kind of man.

Nearly impossible, to be honest.

I ran my fingers through his thick hair, and he moaned softly in his sleep. His eyelashes fluttered ever so slightly, as if he might stir and wake up, but sleep still kept its hold over him.

It was these moments, the quiet, peaceful moments in the middle of the night, that I'd find myself watching him like a creepy little stalker and just savoring him. *My* man. My best friend. The giant who'd managed to fill all the voids I hadn't even known were there until he barreled his way into my life. The man who'd managed to knock down all of my walls and love me for me.

God, I fucking loved him.

I loved him—and our tiny little baby—more than I had ever loved anything in my entire life.

Emotion filled my eyes, and I brushed a few rogue tears off my cheeks. For fuck's sake, I felt like I was always crying. Or about to cry. Or thinking about crying. Or yelling at Thatch for making me cry, even though he had most likely done nothing wrong.

Pregnancy not only made me horny, but it also made me insanely sensitive.

Lately, I'd been a fucking mess over anything and everything. It was exasperating, and sometimes, there wasn't any rhyme or reason for the tears. I mean, all it would take was one Folgers's "Coming Home" commercial, and I'd be two hiccupping breaths away from doing my best impression of that time Kim Kardashian lost her diamond earring in the ocean.

My stomach growled into the still apartment, damn near echoing off the walls, and I glanced over at the clock. Right on schedule, the numbers 1:00 a.m. glowed bright into the darkness of our bedroom. About a week after I found out I was pregnant, every night between the hours of midnight and two, my body had to let its hunger be known.

Word to the wise, pregnancy hunger is on another level of hungry.

Imagine a long workday where you haven't had time for lunch, and by the time three o'clock hits, you're five seconds away from either reenacting The Walking Dead and gnawing your own arm off or considering rummaging through the breakroom fridge without giving a single fuck about eating someone else's food. Now, take that scenario and go into it without eating for about three days. Yes, my friends, that is pregnancy hunger.

A starving pregnant woman should be considered a danger to national security because fuck only knows what we're liable to do if someone doesn't keep us well fed with our outrageous cravings. But we should also be given a free pass because we're the miracle of life, goddammit.

Add some virginity and the baby Jesus and take away my propensity for using the word fuck and I might as well be the Virgin Mary right now.

Literally, the miracle of fucking life.

My stomach rumbled and grumbled again, and I groaned. The last thing I felt like doing was participating in actual movement. While I stared up at the ceiling, perturbed and contemplating how I could teleport a plateful of peanut butter crackers and a glass of strawberry milk into my lap, Thatch shifted his arm from around me, wordlessly got out of bed, and shuffled into the hallway in nothing but his underwear.

I wasn't even sure if he was awake, but I'd wait until I heard anything alarming to send out a search party. And by search party, I meant our mini-pig, Phil.

Five minutes later, Thatch walked back into the bedroom and set a large glass of strawberry milk and a plate with a peanut butter and jelly sandwich on my nightstand. He slid back into bed beside me, kissed my forehead, my lips, and the top swells of each breast that peeked out from my nightshirt, and then adjusted his head on my boobs and whispered, "Love you, honey," as he closed his eyes.

I stared down at him in awe.

Tears pricked my eyes again as I ate my peanut butter and jelly sandwich.

Goddamn him for being so perfect.

More tears filled my eyes and forced a steady stream to slip down my cheeks and onto the side of Thatch's face. And then the sobs took hold, forcing a hiccupping breath and a mouth full of sticky bread crumbs to land in his hair.

Thatch blinked awake and stared up at me, concerned. "Baby? Are you okay?"

I shook my head and didn't even bother wiping away the tears—or the crumbs from my lips.

He sat up, took in my distraught face, and became instantly alarmed. "Cass? What's wrong?"

"You," I wailed.

"Me?"

I nodded. "Yeah. You're too fucking swoony."

He grinned at that. "You're crying because I'm too swoony?"

I nodded again. "You're stupid. And I'm stupid because I love you so goddamn much, you idiot."

He took the plate out of my hands gently, turning just his upper body and setting it on the nightstand. When he shifted back, his hands gripped both of my cheeks and he leaned forward, rubbing his nose against mine. "I love you too, Crazy."

It only made me cry harder.

He chuckled softly and kissed my tear-and-jelly-stained lips.

"I feel like I've turned into Georgia," I whined. "All fudging emotional and fluffing ridiculous. Mother of marshmallows and soup, what is wrong with me?"

"You're pregnant, honey."

"Oh? That's what this is?" I asked in a sarcastic tone and

slapped his chest. He just laughed and rolled onto his back, pulling me with him. "I'm pregnant? Well, son of a sausage biscuit, when did that happen?"

He pressed a soft kiss to my lips, and his warm gaze searched mine. "You're so beautiful, Cass. You take my breath away."

My tear ducts made their presence known and forced more tears to spill from my eyes. "This isn't a game! Stop saying shi-*sneakers* like that to make me cry!"

"Sneakers?"

"Shut your fucking mouth. I've yet to find a good replacement for shit."

He grinned and ran a hand through his hair, but his fingers only made it halfway before they got stuck in the strands coated in PB and J. "Is there food in my hair?"

I shrugged. "Probably."

In true Thatch fashion, he just took it in stride, seemingly more concerned with how my shirt-covered boobs were now pressed against his bare chest than the fact that I had managed to shower him in spit and jelly.

"Goddamn, honeys, did you get bigger overnight?" he asked my tits. And then without warning, he flipped me onto my back and slid the top of my nightshirt down and grabbed both breasts with his big hands, squeezing and groaning his approval. "You did get bigger, my beautiful ladies. You got bigger and softer and, fuck, you're gorgeous." He licked across the top of one and then softly sucked my nipple into his mouth.

I couldn't hide my moan, and he smirked in satisfaction. The conversations he held with my breasts were absurd and insane, but I secretly got off on them in a big way. Especially since they usually ended like this.

His devious tongue moved across to the other nipple and showed it the same appreciation.

My pussy throbbed and my nipples hardened, and I fought the urge to slide my hand into his boxer briefs. "Aren't you tired?" I asked, hiding the breathiness in my voice. "It's like two in the morning. We should probably get some sleep."

"We both know you don't want to sleep right now." He grinned up at me as one big hand skimmed down my belly and into my underwear. His thick finger slid through my arousal until it made its way inside of me. "What time is your flight tomorrow?" His thumb brushed against my clit, and my hips jerked in response.

"Huh?"

He pumped his finger into me deeper. "Your flight? What time is it?"

Flight? He had to be talking about flying his Supercock into my tunnel.

I moaned and started rotating my hips against his hand. "Yes. Put your cock inside me. Fantastic idea."

He smirked. "That's not what I asked, Crazy."

I could have sworn he did, but if he said he didn't, I'd have to take his word for it—and let him know to fucking get where I needed him to go quicker. "Obviously, you're asking the wrong questions."

"You want my cock?" His thumb circled my clit again and applied the perfect amount of pressure to make my toes curl.

My eyes rolled back in my head. "Why are your boxers still on?"

"Are we in the same conversation right now?"

"One of us is having the right conversation. The other one is babbling."

He didn't let up with his magic hands. "Babbling?"

"Thatch," I groaned in frustration, grinding myself against his hand. "Boxers off. Cock inside me. *Now*."

He chuckled and flipped me over onto my belly. One hard slap to my ass urged a squeal from my lips. Before I could offer a snappy retort, he was pulling my panties off my legs and nipping at my ass with his teeth. "My dirty, dirty girl. You'll wait until I'm ready."

Yes. Yes. Yes.

His hands spread my ass cheeks apart as his perfect fucking mouth ate at my pussy from behind. Holy hell. His tongue, his lips, his teeth, he wasn't holding anything back. He moaned against me, tasting every single inch he could reach, and I came hard and fast.

He didn't give me time to come down from climax, flipping me onto my back and spreading my legs wide as he pushed his thick cock inside of me. "Fuck yes," he groaned. "Goddamn, your pussy is gripping me tight."

"Don't stop," I whimpered. "Don't ever fucking stop fucking me, or I swear I will fucking strangle you."

He stopped his momentum and grinned down at me. "And here I thought you had that whole cursing habit kicked."

"Thatch." I glared at him.

"What?" he asked, ironically feigning innocence at the same time my pussy was cradling his dick.

"I swear to God—" I started to say, but my ability to speak coherently came to a quick halt when Thatch kneeled on the bed and lifted me onto his lap, impaling me on his hard and ready Supercock. I straddled his muscular thighs while his big hands gripped my ass.

He thrust his hips up, fast and deep. "This what you want, honey?"

I wanted to mock him by saying no, but my mouth refused to form any words other than, "God, yes."

Stars danced behind my eyelids as he smirked and started a punishing rhythm. "I think you mean, *Thatch, yes*, honey."

Normally, I would've snapped back a sarcastic response, but I was too busy coming all over his cock.

My brain wanted my heart to be angry, but much like in the early stages of our relationship, she completely disagreed.

I love him.

Six, as in six o'fucking clock, came way too early the next morning, and I groaned my disapproval as the alarm blared its annoying reminder that I couldn't let the ungodly hour pass peacefully during REM sleep. Still, old habits die hard.

After I hit snooze for the third time, and blind avoidance was no longer an option, I was lifted out of bed and carried into the bathroom.

"What the hell?" I muttered when the blinding lights of the bathroom had me covering my eyes with both hands.

"Sorry, honey, but you have to get moving if you want to make your flight." Thatch set me down on the bathroom counter and left his warm hands at my hips.

I groaned again. "I'll catch the next flight."

He laughed and reached up slowly, moving my hands away from my eyes with a gentleness I never personally possessed. "Here," he said as he placed a hot mug into my hands. "It's half-caf so you can drink another cup of coffee on the plane."

I lifted the cup to my nose and inhaled my favorite morning aroma while Thatch turned on the shower.

"It's a long way to San Diego. Can I drink two more cups on the plane?"

He turned to me with narrowed eyes. That was his way of saying no without actually saying no. Apparently, I responded better to indirect orders.

I scrunched my nose, but otherwise, put up no more fight. I knew I didn't need to have more than one more cup, and he knew

I knew it. I couldn't even throw it in his face that he got to eat and drink whatever he wanted because it wasn't true. Sure, he could have, but he didn't. When I couldn't have something, he didn't have it either. Sometimes I wondered if he was real.

Steam wisped and weaved above the glass doors, signaling the water was nice and warm. He made his way back to the counter and took the mug from my hands, setting it down and lifting me to my feet. His hands made quick work of my sleep shirt and panties, and before I knew it, he was helping me into the shower.

But when I turned back to put my lips to his, he wasn't there.

"What do you want for breakfast, honey? Eggs and bacon sound good?" he asked, moving toward the bathroom closet.

I just stared at him through the glass and watched him set a towel out for me.

His head tilted to the side. "You okay?"

I opened the shower door and gripped him by the boxer briefs, yanking him off-balance and into the shower with me.

"What the—?"

I wrapped both arms around him and held him tight. "I love you."

His hands found their way into my wet hair, gripping the strands and gently tilting my head back to meet his eyes. He searched my gaze with warmth and love. "I love you too, honey."

Tears pricked my eyes as I buried my face into his chest. "Thank you for being so goddamn sweet."

He chuckled softly. "I'd do anything for you."

I lifted my head. He showed me every fucking day that the words he spoke were true, but I asked anyway. "Anything?"

He nodded, and the little flecks of gold in the center of his chocolate brown eyes bounced and glittered under the bathroom lights. "Anything."

"Fuck me in the shower?"

"I don't want to make you late for your flight, honey, and the things I'm picturing take a whole lot of time." His words said no, but his cock was definitely saying *hell yes* against my belly.

"I guess you better speed them up, then," I responded as I pushed his wet boxer briefs down his legs and started stroking him with my hand.

He smirked, but he didn't resist, lifting me up by my ass and wrapping my legs around his waist. My back was pressed against the tile, and his cock was inside of me between one breath and the next.

The memory of this would stay with me, almost as clear as if he were with me himself, all the way to San Diego and back.

CHAPTER 5

Thatch

"Where are you?" Kline asked, without prompting or greeting, as I put the phone to my ear.

"Your mom's house."

The answer came on instinct and without any planning. Jokes and jabs were where I really excelled, and amiable insults sometimes felt easier than breathing. But my mind wasn't really there, on the unexpected phone call with one of my best friends.

In reality, I could feel the cheap Berber of hotel carpet under my feet, and the sun reflected just slightly off the building across the street. The tinted floor-to-ceiling windows of my room kept it from piercing my eyes like it would have if I'd been outside in it directly, though, and my beard was longer than I'd ever let it get. It was like I was one of those Special Forces guys, highly trained to blend into my surroundings even if it meant acclimating to a completely different culture and becoming a *longhair*. Except, it was actually nothing like that, and the fact that my brain even came up with that analogy just proved how motherfucking insane I was becoming.

"Maureen would be nothing less than disgusted with you right now."

I shook off my self-loathing and focused on the voice in my ear.

"Hey, I didn't mean Maur any disrespect, and I think she knows me well enough to understand that."

He laughed a little, but it was more than an auditory display of mirth. Sort of, *Ha-ha, that Thatch, what a ridiculous fuck.* And really, right now, I agreed with him.

"Trust me, she doesn't."

"Well, fuck. Do I need to worry about Bob hunting me down?" I asked, trying to keep my tone light.

Kline breathed the sigh of the beleaguered. "I was calling to see if you wanted to have lunch. But now I don't think I want to have lunch with you."

"Well, then," I said through a laugh. "I guess it's a good thing I'm not in town then, huh?"

"You're not in town?" I could practically see his eyebrows snapping together in my head. No statement was simple where he was concerned, and frankly, he was right. There was always deeper meaning. He was just better at mining for it than anyone else I knew. "Where the hell are you?"

"Business," I answered as I lifted the binoculars to my eyes and trained them on the building across the street. Then I shook my eyes to clear them when I realized I was too close to need binoculars and set them back on the table to my right.

"Business?" Kline asked, skeptical. "How incredibly fucking vague. I was actually after a location. You know, a state, a country, maybe even a city on Planet Earth."

"I'm busy, okay?" I told him honestly. I didn't plan to tell him much else since I'd pretty much lost my goddamn mind, but I liked

Kline. He deserved at least a little tiny crumb of truth.

"Busy doing what?" he pushed, and then I sighed.

My impatience was about to peak in an all-out musical crescendo.

She was supposed to have been there by now. I'd wanted to follow her the whole way. From her hotel to the supply pickup to the actual shoot, but I'd managed to talk myself out of going full-on paparazzi. That's what made celebrities get into car accidents all the time, and well, that would completely defeat the entire point of everything I'd sunk so low to do.

"I have to go," I told him, and I did. I didn't particularly feel like weeping while I was on the phone with him, and the longer it took Cassie to arrive, the more scenarios of death and carnage and blood passed through my not-well mind. Seriously, this was probably the early stages of a psychotic break, and not at all in keeping with everything I hoped I'd be as a father.

Namely, not a fucking stalker.

Yes, stalking. I'm stalking the soon-to-be mother of my child. Don't say a goddamn word. I know, okay? I know.

"What's going on?" Kline asked again, in that annoying as fuck voice that said he knew everything, and anything he didn't know, he'd find out. *Goddammit.* The cliff above Lose-Your-Fucking-Mind-Burg was already steep, my huge tree-trunk legs walking right along the edge, and he wasn't helping.

"It's nothing, okay?"

"What's nothing? You said it was business," the clever bastard continued, chipping away at me one clue at a time. Next thing I knew, he'd be telling me it was Colonel Thatcher, in the hotel room, with the binoculars.

People shuffled along the busy sidewalk, but I knew she was

supposed to arrive by car, and I knew she was supposed to text me upon her arrival. I'd managed to ask her the details of her shoot and convince her to give me that peace of mind without tipping my hand. Because, trust me, when she got a load of my crazy fucking cards, she wasn't going to be happy. That's why I needed to make sure she never figured it out.

You know, like an honest to God stalker.

Jesus fucking Christ.

"It *is* business," I lied.

His voice was a growl when he asked, "You're not cheating on Cassie, are you? Because I'll fucking kill you with my bare hands."

Yeah, right. Maybe with a cleverly crafted tool and the element of surprise, but not his bare hands. Still.

"No!" Jesus. "No, I'm not cheating on her, okay? I promise, I am *not* cheating on Cassie. I love her." I lowered my voice and muttered under my breath, "Obviously, too much."

"'Then, what the hell is—"

My vision tunneled and my ears completely closed to all conversation as a car with Cassie's beautiful dark locks behind the wheel came to a screeching stop across the street.

"Gotta go!" I managed to snap out before hitting the end button and tossing my phone to the love seat off to my left.

Pressing myself to the windows like a leech, I watched closely as Cassie climbed from the car, a smile on her face and fire in her pretty blue eyes. I couldn't actually see them from this distance, but just from the plump of her cheek, I could tell. I knew everything there was to know about every expression in her arsenal, and this one was all Cassie—sassy, happy, sarcastic as fuck, and everything I'd fallen so hard for in one appealing package.

"God, you fucking animal," I muttered to myself as I watched her lazy fuck of an assistant get out of the car on the other side without a single thing in hand. She'd had to get a new one after firing that cunt, Olivia. Cassie didn't look like she was struggling as she lifted the camera bag over her shoulder, but that didn't matter. I was point five seconds away from homicide. And in my opinion, it was justified.

Cassie spoke highly of the guy, and sure, he looked innocent enough with his button-up shirt and glasses and alarmingly friendly smile, but he wasn't helping a pregnant woman carry shit. So, basically, he was right up there with Lee Harvey Oswald, if you asked me.

Leaning down, Cassie reached into the car, and I caught a glimpse of heaven—or the top swells of her sweet breasts. To me, the two were interchangeable, both mystical wonders created for good little boys by God himself.

But I couldn't concentrate on that like I wanted to because she was reaching into the car for even more things to carry, and it took everything I had not to shoot some sort of Spiderman web out of my hand and bust through the fucking hotel window to swing my way down there.

It's only, like, twenty-five pounds of stuff, max, I tried to remind myself. *She's not going to drop dead on the sidewalk from lifting less than thirty pounds of camera gear. The baby's fine, she's fine, everyone is fucking fine except for you because you're a goddamn psychopath who can't shake this pessimistic doomsday outlook about Cassie's completely healthy pregnancy.*

If I didn't know any better, I'd swear I'd been shot up with all kinds of hormones of my own. I wasn't sure which ones, but they were the kind that made you ripe with paranoia, I guess.

As she disappeared inside the building, I shoved my feet in my shoes sans socks, grabbed my keycard off the table and my phone off the love seat, and jogged for the door.

I'd have to get creative, now that she was actually inside the shoot. Thanks to some careful investigation, done primarily during the middle of sex so her mind would be on other, more cock-like things, I knew the majority of the pictures were to be taken in an outdoor pool. And since I'd scouted the location earlier, I knew there was a restaurant around the back, a block over, with a rooftop deck where said pool was visible. Sure, I wouldn't be in range to do more than dial 911 if she slipped and hit her head and fell into the water and started drowning, but at least I would know.

I was settling my ass into the chair at Want and Waste, an apparently popular San Diego restaurant that served and supported a completely vegan lifestyle, when my phone rang again.

Obviously, I hadn't chosen this place based on cuisine, and I was fairly certain the hostess was on to me, taking in my six-foot-five, two-hundred-and-fifty-pound frame like it was a huge cosmic joke that I was standing in front of her.

I had to agree. Of course, I couldn't eat a fucking burger and fries while I did my stalking, it'd be too damn distracting.

When I unearthed my phone from my pocket, pulled it up in front of the menu, and saw the name, I considered not answering. But I knew that wouldn't help me at all. Detective Kline was officially on the case, and if he'd actually worked for law enforcement, I'd soon be on my way to prison.

Of course, he wanted to fucking FaceTime.

I pushed the button to accept, and his face filled the screen.

"Yes?" I asked with one eyebrow slightly higher than the other.

"Are you at a restaurant?" he asked immediately, taking in the scenery around me like a hawk.

"Yes," I answered honestly. There was no reason to lie about something he could quite clearly see for himself.

"By yourself?"

"Yes," I said with a laugh. "I'm not cheating on Cassie. Even if I could consider the possibility of cheating on her, I'd never cheat on her tits. Never."

"Christ," Kline groaned and scrubbed at his face as a couple at the table in front of me turned my way.

Whoops. "Sorry," I told them with a wince.

Okay, so it was more of a wink than a wince, but this is me we're talking about.

I chanced a peek over toward the building where she was working, the crystal water of the pool sparkling in the early afternoon sun. There was a flurry of activity, but Cassie stood off to the side, her head bent over her phone.

The text message notification sounded on my phone.

"Hold on," I told Kline, tapping my way out of the call screen and pulling up my messages.

Cassie's Tits: I'm here, but you probably already know that.

She's on to me.

My lungs seized, the air in them freezing in panic.

"Motherfucking shit," I breathed, forgetting that Kline could still see me and that the people at the table in front of me were the goddamn language police.

"What?" Kline asked, but I was busy fake apologizing to the people five feet away with sticks up their asses.

"Thatch," Kline called, annoyed about having anything other than my undivided attention. "What's going on?"

But I had a woman to worry about right now. Knowing what

usually worked best, I went with ignorance.

Me: Huh?

She responded almost immediately. Thank God.

***Cassie's Tits: I know you printed out my schedule, and I
know you know I was supposed to be here thirty minutes ago.
I'm impressed you managed to resist the urge to text me first,
though.***

Jesus Christ. If she only knew.

Me: Ha. I love you.

Probably past the point of what's healthy, I admitted to myself.

Cassie's Tits: I love you too.

"Thatch!" Kline called.

"Goddammit. Give me a motherfucking second here, Kline-
hole," I muttered, and finally disgusted, the people at the table in
front of me pushed out of their chairs and left. Granted, their food
had been consumed and the bill paid, but I was pretty sure I was
the real catalyst for their retreat.

"Fine," Kline agreed over the speaker. "I don't think you're
where the answers really are anyway."

Shit. It was *not* a good sign that he was giving up this easily.

"Enjoy your lunch in… Where did you say you were again?"

"I didn't."

Out of my messages and back on the call, I watched as he
smiled.

"Enjoy San Diego," he said with a glimmer in one of his stupid blue eyes. And then he was gone.

Goddammit.

CHAPTER 6

Cassie

The bags of takeout rustled lightly as I set them on the kitchen counter and headed into our bedroom to change out of the clothes I flew home in.

The second my flight landed at JFK, I grabbed a taxi and got to work on setting my evening plans into motion. Since I was a little surprised Thatch wasn't home by now, I shot him a quick text as I headed back into the kitchen.

> *Me: Where are you?*
> *Thatch: Just now leaving the office. You make it home, okay?*

As I tied the strap of my frilly apron around my waist, I glanced at the clock on the stove and noted it was half past eight. I found it a little odd that he was just now leaving work.

> *Me: Yep. I'm home. You're still at work???*
> *Thatch: No use coming home to an empty apartment,*

honey. ;)

Charming motherfuc—fluffer. Thatch's suggestion that I clean up my language hadn't really sunk in until it had been reinforced by suggestions from Georgia, Winnie, my mom, my brother, and the lady at the grocery store. Though, the lady at the grocery store hadn't known I was pregnant, so she was just an uptight cunt.

There was a lot of time left before it became a real issue, but evidence was suggesting it was going to take every single minute of it to reform.

Me: What about coming home to me in an apron and stilettos?
Thatch: Naked dinner?
Me: ;)
Thatch: You know you get spanked for stealing my signature winks.
Me: ;) ;) ;) ;)
Thatch: I do love your ass when it's really fucking pink.
Me: You know what else is nice and pink?
Thatch: Tell me.
Me: My pussy.
Thatch: I think you mean MY pussy.
Me: ;)
Thatch: 10 minutes, honey. Be ready.

I grinned at how easily he played into my hands—not that I'd expected him to resist. I set my phone on the counter, and started removing the Chinese takeout containers from the brown paper bag.

What? This is my version of making dinner.

I lit the candles on the dining room table and dressed up the takeout dishes by tossing them in our nicest serving platters. Thatch knew I wasn't Susie Homemaker, and there wasn't a chance in hell I would actually cook a meal, but he always appreciated when I went above and beyond. And if I was being honest, and not the least bit humble, the whole scene was pretty enough to post from Martha Stewart's Instagram account—*which just goes to show, you really can fake fucking anything.*

Naked dinners, our Wednesday night ritual, were one of Thatch's favorite things. But since I had been out of town for the past two Wednesdays, I had some serious making up to do.

True to his word, ten minutes later, Thatch strolled through the door and met me in the kitchen with a giant-ass grin on his face. "Hi, honey," he said as his eyes trailed over the sight of me in nothing but a frilly apron and black stilettos. "There is literally nothing better than coming home to you like this."

I smiled and gave him a little twirl, showing off my bare ass in the process.

His grin grew wider as he moved toward me. "God, I'm a lucky son of a bitch."

I nodded my head, and he chuckled. "Modesty becomes you."

Thatch didn't waste any time, lifting me into his arms and wrapping my legs around his waist. He buried his nose in my neck and inhaled deeply, whispering, "Mmm, you always smell so good." He leaned back and took my mouth in a soft and sweet kiss while his hands continued to palm my ass and squeeze the pliant flesh playfully. Heat consumed the kiss and me, making a greedy ache take over low in my belly as Thatch grinded himself against me with a deep groan. "Fuck, I missed you."

I giggled against his lips. "Me too. But not enough that I won't suspend you from naked dinners if you don't get to work on losing the clothes."

He chuckled and set me on the kitchen counter. "Suspended? Please, tell me what exactly you'd do without me at naked dinner."

I shrugged. "Probably just rub one out on the kitchen table."

"I meant for you to tell me in detail…painfully explicit, one or two fingers, what you taste like, detail," he told me through a smile as he pulled off his clothes. With a flick of one red-tipped finger, I motioned for him to give me a spin, and he playfully obliged, shaking his bare ass in my direction. I laughed and hopped off the kitchen counter, spanking the meat of one taut cheek before heading into the dining room.

He sat down at the table, and I served him his favorite meal from Wok-n-Roll: Kung Pao Chicken with a side of egg roll. As I spooned Shrimp Lo Mein onto my plate, I noticed Thatch's expression was less playful and more serious as his gaze honed in on my stomach.

"What's wrong, T?"

"Does your assistant help you carry shit when you're on location?"

My brow furrowed. "Carry what? My camera bag? Pretty sure I can manage that, honey."

He shook his head. "Does he help you?"

I shrugged. "Sure, I guess."

Thatch grabbed the knot of my apron and pulled me toward him. He untied the strings and tossed the frilly material haphazardly onto the floor. His hands gripped my waist and he leaned forward, softly kissing my belly. "Promise me something, honey."

Confusion made my face tense up, but somehow, I knew this wasn't the time to tease him about not making sense. Instead, I rested my hands on his bare shoulders, rubbing at the smooth, hot skin with the pads of my thumbs. "What's that?"

"Promise me that you'll ask for help more when you're out of town. Ask your lazy-ass assistant to help you carry shit, okay? It's his job to assist you. That includes doing all of the menial shit like carrying your camera bag."

I tilted my head to the side and stared down at him. "I think you're being a little flipping dramatic, Thatcher. I mean, I'm not that far along. I'm not even showing at this point."

He kissed my belly again. "Yeah, but one day you will be show-ing. I just want you to get used to asking for help. Sometimes you can be a little stubborn about shit like that." He glanced up at me, and I scrunched my face in annoyance.

God, he was being weird tonight.

"Please, Cass."

Normally, I wouldn't have backed down without a little more of a fight, but I could tell by the pleading look in his big brown eyes that this wasn't something he was taking lightly.

"It's that important to you?"

"You and our little baby will always be my top priority."

"Fine, honey. I'll try to be a lot lazier when I'm on location and make people do more things for me. Hell, maybe I'll add a cabana boy and a few half-naked men who are scheduled to feed me pick-les and fan me with giant leaves every thirty minutes to my rider."

"Thank you."

I kissed his forehead and set my plate beside his. I sat down in his lap, and he hissed his approval when his hard cock nestled between my ass cheeks. "I love your seating arrangements for this naked dinner. I think we should go ahead and assign seats for the year."

"I figured you'd enjoy it." I grabbed my fork and started to dig into my food.

But Thatch had other plans. His hands grazed the bare skin of my sides until they reached the bottom swells of my breasts and then went back, repeating the maddening circuit until my nipples hardened and my hips started to move of their own accord, shifting and rotating and desperately searching for relief from the constant throbbing ache that had taken up residence below my belly.

His hands gripped my hips, stopping their momentum, and shifting me so that his cock was now snuggled against where I was slick with arousal. I moaned and set my fork down. My fingers clung to the edge of the table as I begged for him to slide inside of me.

"You don't want to eat first, honey?"

"Unless, by eating, you mean your mouth on my pussy, then no. I don't want to eat first."

Thatch's hand swept across the dining room table, and dishes clanged to the floor in the span of a heartbeat. My back hit the table next, and my thighs were spread and resting on his shoulders a few seconds later.

"Of course, that's what I meant." He smirked like the devil. "It's been four days since I've had my mouth on you, and I refuse to let another minute pass without the taste of your pussy on my tongue."

He buried his face between my thighs at the same time his big hands reached up and caressed my breasts. My back arched off the table when he nipped my clit with his teeth and then sucked the sting better with his hot mouth.

"Oh, fuck."

"You taste so good, honey." He moaned against me like I was the most delicious thing he'd ever feasted on. A few rhythmic flicks of his tongue and my climax came so hard, so fast, that I felt dizzy with the insane pleasure that took ahold of all of my senses.

My body was still shaking as he stood between my thighs and drove his cock inside me. When he lifted my legs to rest on his shoulders, the position felt so deliciously intense that I quickly sucked in a breath through my teeth at the tight feel of him filling me.

"You like this, baby?"

"God, yes. It feels so good, Thatch."

He circled his hips. "I'll never get tired of how good you feel wrapped around me." The rhythm of our skin slapping together started out slow and low, and he kept it up until both of us were barely breathing through mismatched, ragged pants and moans were spilling from my lips. He moved his hand between my breasts and down, past my stomach, until his fingers reached the place where our bodies joined. His thumb circled my clit in the same tempo as his hips. I whimpered as I felt myself slowly unravel at the seams.

"Yes, Cass," he hissed. "You're so fucking close. I can feel your pussy starting to fist my cock."

I didn't need him to tell me I was there to know that I was, and he knew that just as well as I did. But those words spoken harshly, like he was right there too, pushed me even further.

My head fell back onto the table, and my eyes fell closed as my climax built to a point of no return. I cried out as Thatch fucked me harder and faster and filled me so deep I felt like I didn't know where he ended and I began.

"Fuck," he shouted and pounded out his release inside of me.

Once our breaths slowed and we both regained the ability for coherent speech, Thatch slid his hands behind my back and pulled me into his arms as he sat back down in the chair behind him.

He held me like that for a long moment, his lips softly kissing my shoulder, my neck, my jaw, and my lips.

"I think we're going to have to order pizza for naked dinner now," I whispered into his ear. "No doubt our Chinese food is cold."

"You know, there's this thing called a microwave…"

"Shut up, smartass," I retorted. "And since most of our food is now on the floor, I'm in the mood for pizza instead."

"Are you in the mood to clean this mess up, too?"

"*Hell.* No," I scoffed. "Rule number 235, Thatcher. You make the mess. *You* clean it up."

"I thought that rule only applied to cum shots on your stomach."

I leaned back and raised an eyebrow. "Oh, please, tell me the last time you actually pulled out."

His fingers trailed across my slightly rounded lower abdomen and a soft, easy grin consumed his mouth. "It's been awhile."

"Yeah. *Awhile.*" I laughed and tapped him on the nose with my index finger. "You clean. I'll order pizza."

"Okay. Fine." He chuckled. "Wanna take a shower first?"

I nodded and slid out of his lap. "Netflix and pizza in bed?"

"Brilliant plan, honey. Especially if there's another silent 'chill' in there."

He followed me into our bedroom, and I winked over my shoulder. His answering smile made my knees feel weak.

While Thatch greeted a sleepy Phil, who refused to get up from his bed, I flipped on the shower and set out some towels. "Oh, I forgot to tell you," I called out from the bathroom. "I had to reschedule the shoot in Seattle."

"When is it now?"

"Saturday."

"Next Saturday? I thought that was the Mavericks shoot in Phoenix?" he asked and met my gaze in the bathroom mirror. A few weeks ago, Georgia had asked that I join the team on an away game and shoot a pictorial for their new marketing materials. Of course, I'd said yes, even though I knew it was going to add an additional level of traveling hell to my schedule. But I'd be with Georgia and Winnie, flying into Phoenix on the team jet and earning some downtime with the girls when I wasn't shooting. Silver lining for sure.

"No." I shook my head and proceeded to brush out the knots

in my hair. "This Saturday is Seattle now, next Saturday will be Phoenix."

His brow furrowed. "You're leaving again in less than forty-eight hours?"

"Unfortunately, yes." I set my brush on the counter and turned to face him. "It was the only way to fit the shoot in."

I sensed his frustration and moved toward him, wrapping my arms around his waist and placing a soft kiss on his chest. "Don't worry, honey. I'll make sure you have plenty of time to fuck my brains out before I leave again."

I glanced up at him, and he quirked a brow. "Better you than me," he murmured, almost to himself. "These days, I'm not sure I have all that many brain cells left to waste."

CHAPTER 7

Wes

Head down with my chin to my chest to protect against the chilly October wind, I moved swiftly from the hired town car to my plane and jogged up the stairs. Tonight, I was headed out to Phoenix for Sunday's away game.

My personal flight attendant, Janine, stood waiting to greet me as I ducked through the door. "You're the last one, Mr. Lancaster," she told me with a smile.

"Well, nothing new there, huh?" I replied easily because it was true.

I knew it wasn't fair to the people waiting for me, but I'd made quite the name for myself in the being-late department. There always seemed to be just one more person waiting to talk to me about some issue or some phone call to answer. A last-minute email asking for staff approval or a change to the menu at BAD. A fight between chef and sous-chef and what I wanted to do about it, and if I liked the blue or the red lights for the bar makeover.

There was always *something* that needed attention, and most of the time, I loved it. I loved to be busy and needed, and it made me feel good to put so much time and input into everything I did. But there really weren't enough waking hours in the day, and because of that, I was always fifteen minutes late. Always.

Three sets of blue eyes hit me like a wave of water as I turned to the cabin and took a step forward.

All three women looked at me in their own way, but they all managed to say the same terrifying thing without actually speaking the words aloud: *I've been designed to bring a man to his knees.*

"Christ. I definitely didn't think this through," I muttered with a cheeky grin. "I should have flown commercial."

Georgia was the first to move, jumping up to greet me with a friendly hug. She laughed through it and then pulled back to look me in the eyes. "Aw, come on, Wesley. Three big, bad girls scare you enough to brave the wilds of commercial air travel?"

"Yes," Frankie Hart, my GM for the Mavericks, mumbled from the other side of the aisle, but he was smiling when all of our eyes shifted to him. "Just kidding."

Cassie's and Winnie's contempt melted into contentment like chocolate on a hot day.

Georgia's smile never wavered. She'd known Frankie longer, and she liked him and his good-natured humor enough to call him Uncle Frankie on occasion.

It freaked me out a little, but I think that was mostly because I'd never gotten to know him on anything more than a professional level.

And whose fault is that?

As Frankie put earbuds in his ears and opened his laptop to old game footage, Georgia dragged me over to sit with her and the women. I looked over my shoulder at Frankie and his laptop longingly. He was kind enough to spend only five seconds silently laughing at me.

Janine walked the aisle from the back of the plane to the front and asked all of us to fasten our seatbelts. I settled in and did as she asked, swiping the screen of my phone to unlock it and getting lost in the land of correspondence rather than becoming the fourth hen in the coop.

They filled the silence with mindless chatter about shoes and skirts and hair color and something godawful called Jamberry Nails, as we taxied out onto the runway and turned into position for takeoff. The engines roared as the pilot throttled forward, and I cracked my neck back and forth a couple of times to fight off a kink.

The fall air lifted us up and into the sky easily enough, and a piercing ray from the setting sun hit my eye like a laser.

Winnie didn't say much, as though she was content to let the Georgia and Cassie duo do most of the talking. I glanced in her direction a couple of times, but I avoided eye contact carefully. It felt safer to follow the line of her silky legs as they disappeared under her skirt or count the number of times her stiletto-clad toe tapped the carpeted floor.

I wasn't looking to get caught, no matter what I was looking at, so after giving myself the opportunity to make a full-body circuit twice, I turned my attention back to my phone.

Well. Except for my ears. They were still highly trained on the babbling conversation of three beautiful women.

"Who's watching Lexi?" Cassie asked, and I couldn't stop myself from peeking up from the email I was typing to glance at Winnie.

I knew she had a kid, but I tried not to think about it.

And yes, I'm well aware that makes me sound like an asshole. But remember how busy I said I am? Kids take all kinds of time and energy. Not in the bad way, they just deserve someone who can give them everything. Every effort, countless moments, and endless encouragement. I'm the guy who would show up fifteen minutes late to the recital—if at all.

I fucking knew the kid complicated going there, but my dick didn't want to hear it. He wanted her—*I wanted her*—and ignoring the kid seemed like the only acceptable compromise, for the time being.

"My brother Remy," she answered easily, and my half-assed attention immediately kicked into overdrive.

Remy. *Her brother.*

She'd pretty easily left out that little detail when I'd had my tantrum in her office. I'd tried pretty hard to lock it down, but I'd been instantly jealous at the sight of another guy's name on her phone.

I'm insane. It's not like she belongs to me.

"Does Remy watch her a lot?" Georgia asked, but my mind turned down the volume on her voice and started to run through its own commentary.

Jesus. I needed to remind myself of a few things here. Kids were fucking sticky and needy and always had a knack for interrupting all pleasurable activities with the need to shit, vomit, or exercise some other disgusting bodily function.

You don't need a goddamn woman with a kid. No matter how fucking sexy she is.

Her white shirt looked crisp against her tan skin, and the dusky gray-blue of her eyes flicked to me on more than one occasion. Georgia and Cassie didn't seem to notice, too busy cackling and laughing with one another, but I sure did.

My cock was half hard behind the fly of my pants.

Jam hands, I told myself. *Remember that kids always have sticky goddamn jam hands.*

"It's usually Remy," Winnie went on, and my ears perked back up at the rough rasp of her authoritative voice. "If not him, one of my other brothers is usually free."

How many fucking brothers did she have?

"How many fucking brothers do you have?" Cassie asked, and I nearly seized up at the realization that crazy Cassie Phillips and I were traveling the same road of thinking.

Though, hers probably had considerably fewer visualizations of Winnie's naked body on all the billboards.

Winnie's laugh rang in my ears. "Four. Remy, Jude, Ty, and Flynn."

"Fucking hell. One shy of a basketball team," Cassie commented, and Georgia's eyebrows pulled together as if she was mentally trying to figure out if Cassie was correct. I laughed at that.

"What?" Winnie asked me. Her voice was hard, no doubt thinking I was laughing at her.

I jerked my chin toward Georgia. "Little Georgie. Working for the NFL and still no concept of sports."

"I know about football," Georgia muttered.

Cassie added, "Sort of," and we all laughed.

My interest returned to Winnie quickly enough, scanning from her crossed legs all the way up to her eyes. "What happens when none of your brothers can watch her?" I found myself asking.

What the fuck, Wes? This doesn't sound like ignoring the existence of the kid to me.

Winnie answered me, but she looked at Cassie as she did. "I have a regular nanny. But she's also a full-time student, so my brothers fill in the holes."

"I bet they fill lots of holes," Cassie said to everyone's amusement but Winnie's.

She groaned. "Don't you dare put that goddamn picture in my head."

"We'll watch her sometime," Cassie volunteered once she

stopped laughing. "We could use the practice."

"She's not like the sample cart at the grocery store," I grumbled. Three very active sets of eyes swung to me again.

Shit.

But Winnie's eyes—openly surprised and unexpectedly warm—were the only ones I could seem to see.

CHAPTER 8

Winnie

I stared out the window, watching the white, bubbly clouds float past as we slid through blue sky. The sun had already set over the horizon, highlighting my aerial view in hues of reds and oranges and pinks. With Georgia and Cassie running the gab show, the flight had been nothing short of entertaining, despite my mind's incessant need to fixate on every single thing about the tall, handsome, irritatingly surly man sitting across the aisle. It felt like every two minutes or so my brain urged my eyes to chance a glance in Wes's direction.

I'd never considered myself anything less than intelligent, but on this matter, the one that revolved around my hidden desire for Wes Lancaster, I was two more secret glances away from being a certified idiot.

He was not the kind of man a woman with a six-year-old daughter should ever want to get involved with.

But he is the kind of man you enjoy mind-numbing, wild, hot, insanely dirty sex with…

Before I let myself board that train of thought, I checked the time and realized we would be landing in Phoenix shortly. Since I knew the pilot would be calling for everyone to turn off their mobile devices in the next ten minutes, I made a quick call to Remy to see how things were going back home.

The phone rang three times before he picked up, and I glanced around the cabin to find everyone else pretty much occupied with their own devices.

"Hey, Win," he greeted.

"I figured I'd call and see how things were going. How's Lex?" I asked and tapped the screen to put his voice on speaker because, yeah, no one was paying attention to my boring conversation, and I was too damn lazy to hold the phone up to my ear. First world problems, right?

"She's good, Win. I just put her to bed, and she was out before I finished reading the Mavericks' offensive stats for their game against Phoenix last year."

I laughed and shook my head. "I told her no football stats at bedtime."

He chuckled. "Yeah, well, Uncle Remy didn't tell her that, and Mom's not home. Anyway, I'm pretty sure she knows more about football now than I do. When did she get so interested in the NFL?"

"Since I took the job with the Mavericks," I explained. My six-year-old daughter had a tendency to fixate on things. Once she had the voracious urge to learn something new, she'd use all of her brainpower to absorb and devour anything and everything related to it.

"I'm still trying to figure out how half of Nick's genes make up Lexi. She's so fucking smart, Win. Are you sure she's Nick's daughter?" Rem asked with a teasing tone.

There was no denying my brother Remy—actually, all four of my brothers—despised Lexi's father with a passion. But it was par for the course, considering our nasty breakup and Nick's tendency to be MIA.

I laughed. "Unfortunately, yes. And you act like her dad is a moron. He runs the neurosurgery department at one of the most prestigious hospitals in the country, Rem. That's about as far from moron as you can get."

"Don't defend him."

I sighed. "I'm not defending him."

"Yeah, you are." His voice had taken on a serious edge. One that was very uncalled for, but it was expected when it came to anything related to Nick Raines. "Are you guys dating again or something?"

Deep down, me getting back together with Nick was Remy's biggest fear. I honestly thought he'd be happy if I just remained single and focused on my daughter and work for the rest of my life. He was ridiculous, but I knew he was just worried and trying to live up to the role of protective older brother.

But I wasn't a child. I was a grown-ass woman who could handle her own shit, and considering I'd managed to finish my residency while pregnant with Lexi, I'd say I had been successful so far.

"Win," he added sternly. "Is there something you're not telling me?"

"Jesus, Rem. Not that it's any of your business, but I'm not dating Nick. That ship sailed about six years ago."

"Oh, really? So what about last year? Why did *that* happen, knowing that ship had sailed?"

My face flamed red, and my jaw damn near fell into my lap. How in the hell did Remy know about that one wine-fueled night with Nick?

I chanced a glance around the cabin to see if anyone caught that part of our conversation, but luckily, Frankie, Cass, and Georgia still had their earbuds in, and Wes's nose was buried in his laptop. I flipped the phone off speaker and held it to my ear. "Who told you about that?"

"Ty."

"*What?* When did he tell you that? Seriously, how did that subject even manage to come up?"

"Tonight, when he stopped by to hang out with me and Lex," he explained. "Nick called to say hello, and Ty hopped on the phone and gave him a piece of his mind."

Thanks a lot, Ty. Consider yourself officially scratched off the one and only brother I can confide in list.

"You guys do realize I'm not sixteen, right?" I sighed heavily, and my eyes rolled skyward. "I swear to God, I'm never telling you guys anything. You're like a bunch of gossiping high school girls hopped up on steroids and ready to join the wrestling squad," I muttered into the receiver.

"Look, Win, I'm not trying to be a dick here. I just don't want to see you or Lexi get hurt. A man who can't even make it to his daughter's birthday, *two years in a fucking row*, is a moron *and* an asshole. Lex doesn't deserve that bullshit, and neither do you."

I couldn't disagree with him there, but Remy's tendency to protect us was unwarranted. I wasn't their teenage baby sister anymore. I was an adult who could make her own decisions, and my track record of making the right decisions for my daughter was spotless.

"Good thing she's got four uncles who more than make up for it," I said, trying my best to lighten the tone and direction of the conversation. The last thing I felt like doing was discussing my sex life—*or lack thereof*—with my brother. "And even though it's really none of your concern, I have zero plans for letting something like that happen again, Rem. It was just one night, fueled by too much wine, that happened a very long time ago."

I breathed a sigh of relief when the pilot announced over the intercom that we were about to land. I was more than ready to cut this phone call short. "Hey, we're about to land. I'll call you tomorrow, okay? Give Lexi a kiss for me." Before Rem could interrogate me further, I ended the call and slipped my phone back into my purse.

As our plane started to slowly descend toward the ground, I looked across the cabin to find Wes staring back at me. Our eyes locked for a brief moment before I looked away and silently prayed he hadn't heard the part of my conversation that insinuated nefarious things with my ex-boyfriend Nick. Why I even cared about that was still open for debate. Because honestly, why did I care what Wes heard? Frankly, it was none of his business either.

"Your brother has a fuckhot voice, Win." Cassie's comment pulled my eyes away from the window and back toward the cabin.

"*What?*" I asked with a laugh.

"Remy has a sexy as fuck voice," she answered with a smirk.

My nose scrunched up in disgust. "He's my brother, Cass. There will never be a time in my life where I equate the word sexy with him."

"But what about your other three brothers? For the love of God, tell me they sound just like Remy."

Georgia groaned. "Here we go."

"What? I can't acknowledge a sexy voice?"

Georgia pointed in Cassie's direction. "This has zero to do with his voice and everything to do with the fact that he's Win's *brother.*"

Cassie tilted her head to the side. "You think I've got a thing for brothers?"

Georgia nodded. "Yes. My brother Will is Exhibit A for that case. It should also be noted that I think you need to stop reading so many stepbrother romance novels."

I laughed at that, not the least bit surprised Cassie had a thing for that romance trope. Her book choices generally cracked me

up. If they weren't BDSM-based, they were quick and dirty—
one-handed reads, if you know what I'm saying.

The plane jolted a few times as the wheels hit the runway, and
the brakes squealed when the pilot worked to bring all of our forward momentum to rest.

"Wait… Stepbrother romance novels?" Wes asked while the
plane taxied down the runway. "That's a thing?"

"It's a thing, Wes," Cass explained. "A very hot thing."

Georgia's nose scrunched up. "It's gross."

Cassie rolled her eyes. "They're not related. It's not incest."

"You're deranged. A total fucking pervert," Georgia teased
with a smirk.

"Thank you." Cass grinned and then looked at Wes. "You got
a brother, Wes?"

He shook his head and laughed. "Nope."

"Damn," she muttered.

"You're with Thatch, you freak," Georgia said. "And you also
happen to be knocked up with his child."

Cass smirked. "Pregnancy makes me horny, and I'm traveling
so much I barely get to see him. Spank bank material is needed.
Anyway, I know Thatch jerks off to Margot Robbie when I'm not
home. He can't get e-fucking-nough of her since we saw *Suicide
Squad*."

"She was so badass as Harley Quinn," I tossed out.

"Right?" Cass agreed. "You should be her for Halloween, Win.
You'd make a hot Harley Quinn."

I laughed. "Pretty sure my neighbors wouldn't be thrilled with
me strolling around in booty shorts while Lex goes door-to-door."

"Yeah, but you could wear that costume to Brooks Media's big
Halloween bash," she encouraged with a waggle of her brows.

"Oh, yeah! You have to go to that, Win. It's a blast," Georgia
exclaimed. "Plus, my usual drinking partner got knocked up, so

I'm looking for a new one." She flashed a wink at Cassie and earned a middle finger in return.

"When is it?"

"Three weeks from this Saturday," Georgia said. "We're playing Baltimore at home, so we'll be in town."

I glanced at the calendar on my phone and noted zero prior obligations. "Count me in. I'll find someone to keep Lexi overnight."

Georgia fist-pumped the air as the pilot announced our successful arrival in Phoenix over the intercom and instructed us that we could now get out of our seats and depart from the plane.

Everyone stood, and Georgia made a point of glaring at Cass. "By the way, Cass, that was total TMI about your spank bank. I'd like to keep my appetite for dinner, thank you very much."

Cassie just laughed it off and grabbed her purse from beneath her seat. "Speaking of dinner, where are you taking us, Wes?"

He scrunched his brows together. "Huh?"

Cassie slid her purse over her shoulder and confidently announced, "You're taking us to dinner tonight, Lancaster."

He tilted his head to the side, and an amused smirk kissed his lips. "I am?"

She nodded. "Yep. You're paying, and you're also taking us somewhere I can eat a steak the size of Thatcher's head."

"You have to get your steak well done, Cassie," Georgia chimed in.

"Fluffing pregnancy police," she mumbled and walked down the aisle and off the plane.

Wes motioned for me to slip into the aisle before him with a soft smirk. "You coming to dinner with us?"

I shrugged one of my shoulders. "I'm not sure I have a choice."

He chuckled softly. "That makes two of us."

I glanced back to shoot an amused smile in his direction, and

I didn't miss the fact that his gaze had now honed in on my ass. He was *literally* staring at my ass, and when he looked up and met my eyes, he just grinned. Not the least bit ashamed he had been caught red-handed.

What the hell?

Wes's taste in dining was impeccable. He had taken us to a swanky joint called Red that was only a few miles from our hotel. It was an upscale restaurant that literally lived up to its name. The lights, the walls, the décor, pretty much everything in the room was a different shade of red. What should have reminded me of horror flicks like *Carrie* or *The Shining*, only gave a warm ambiance of fine dining and quiet charm.

About twenty minutes after we had checked in to our hotel, Wes had managed to reserve a table for us at Red and even had a car waiting to escort us when everyone was ready to go. The man might have been consistently late to pretty much everything, but he sure as shit could get things done when they mattered most.

And trust me, with a hungry pregnant woman in the group, food is more important than everything else.

In record time, and much to Cass's excitement and pregnancy cravings, we were sitting at a table in the back of the restaurant and enjoying our meals. Her propensity for keeping the conversation moving and shaking was quickly quelled once her giant, *albeit well-done*, steak was set before her.

I ate my lobster risotto until I felt too full to continue and proceeded to work on my third glass of stupidly expensive wine, courtesy of Wes Lancaster. I knew I was a bit of a lightweight when it came to alcohol, but I couldn't deny this was probably the best Pinot Noir I had ever tasted in my life.

While I drank, and everyone else ate, I couldn't stop fixating on this nagging thought that had been in my brain since I got off the plane. Had Wes really been staring at my ass? And why in the hell did he not even attempt to avert his eyes?

I felt like he wanted me to know he was looking, which only confused me more. I mean, this was a man whose disdain for me was evident in most of our interactions.

I was mindfucked and far too emboldened by alcohol to stop myself from finding answers. Throwing caution to the wind—well, the wine, really—I took my phone out of my purse and typed out a text.

Me: Were you really staring at my ass on the plane?

I watched Wes as he pulled his phone out of his pocket and scanned my text. His brow furrowed, and he met my eyes from the across the table as he typed out a response.

Wes: I have no idea what you're talking about, Dr. Winslow.

Bullshit. I raised a questioning brow in his direction, and he appeared unfazed as I tapped out my rebuttal.

Me: Yeah, you do.

He grinned once my message reached his phone.

Wes: Do you want me to stare at your ass?

His gaze turned cocky, and it took all of my willpower not

to reach across the table and smack him. Instead of drawing the attention of everyone in the room with an outrageous display of violence, I chose the next best thing.

> *Me: No. And it's completely unprofessional to say something like that, Mr. Lancaster.*
> *Wes: Is it unprofessional when you're staring at my ass as well?*

He was calling my bluff. There was no way he knew I had a secret fetish for watching his perfectly toned and damn near bitable ass. I was far too covert during my ass-ogle missions…*right?*

> *Me: I do not stare at your ass.*
> *Wes: It's okay, sweetheart. I don't mind.*
> *Me: This feels like sexual harassment.*
> *Wes: I'm pretty sure you started this conversation.*
> *Me: Only because I caught you memorizing the curves of my ass like there was going to be a pop quiz on it later.*
> *Wes: And your legs.*

Aha! I *knew* it. I couldn't stop a satisfied smile from cresting my lips, but I hated the fact that my enjoyment over his response had nothing to do with proving him wrong. I *liked* that he had been checking me out. Far too much, if I was truly being honest with myself.

> *Me: That is so inappropriate.*
> *Wes: Those sexy fucking heels and skirts you prance around in are the only things that are inappropriate.*

I looked up from my phone and found him smiling smugly

in my direction. My eyes shot a death glare as I typed out another response.

Me: I do not prance.

He nodded.

Wes: You prance.

God, I hated how pleased he looked with himself. That smug smile would've looked better covered in a plateful of my lobster risotto.

Me: Could your suits be any tighter by the way?
Wes: I could have my tailor make some adjustments if that's something you'd enjoy.
Me: You look ridiculous. Like you're two breaths away from your muscles ripping the seams.
Wes: You like my muscles?
Me: No. It's completely unattractive to be that ripped.
Wes: So, it's safe to say Nick is more beanpole in comparison?

My brow furrowed. How in the hell did he know about Nick? I met his persistent gaze until the lightbulb went off...*my phone call with Remy on the plane.*

Me: Eavesdropping on my conversations is rude.
Wes: You were on speakerphone, sweetheart. You made that conversation everyone on the plane's business.
Me: It's even ruder to point that out.
Wes: Tell me, Winnie. What happened a year ago?
Me: None of your fucking business.

I could feel Wes's eyes on me as I set my phone down on the table and did my best to avoid speaking with him, hell, even looking at him, for the rest of the evening. I knew that was the best decision. My track record with wine and attraction to men who were bad news was not good.

What happened a year ago? I mean, seriously? That was none of his concern. And why would he even ask that question? He had no right to know anything about my dating life…or lack thereof.

God, he was infuriating. I could feel my blood boil beneath my skin as I scowled at Wes over my glass of wine.

Georgia and Cassie continued a conversation about the sex of the baby, seemingly unaware of the damn near suffocating tension hovering between Wes and me. How they missed it was a miracle. The air had grown so thick I felt the urge to reach up and cut through it with Cassie's steak knife.

Wes held my irritated stare but seemed more amused by it than anything else. "Do you like the wine, Winnie?" he asked in a tone that would've sounded sweet to everyone else's ears.

But I knew better. He was being a condescending prick.

My inner bitch immediately unsheathed her claws, all too ready to knock his ego down a few pegs.

I shrugged and schooled my facial expression into neutral. "It's okay, I guess. Not necessarily worth five hundred a bottle, but it'll do."

He chuckled. "What is that? Your *third* glass?"

I rolled my eyes, and Cassie groaned. "I wish I could drink three glasses of wine right now."

"No wine allowed, Casshead," Georgia quickly interrupted.

"Shut. Up," Cass retorted with a glare that would've had most people averting eye contact in hopes of self-preservation. Of course, Georgia wasn't the least bit intimated. She might have been tiny, but that girl possessed one hell of a fight inside of her when it came to something she felt strongly about. And keeping Cassie and the baby healthy had recently become one of her top priorities. To the point of annoyance for everyone around her.

"You know, one glass wouldn't hurt you or the baby, Cassie," I offered.

Georgia's eyes practically shot laser beams in my direction. "Winnie! Do not encourage her to drink alcohol."

Cassie flipped Georgia off. "Can someone take the pregnancy police home? She's a total fluffing fun ruiner."

"Who's the pregnancy police?"

We all turned in the direction of the deep male voice to find Kline smirking down at our table.

Cassie pointed to Georgia. "Your wife. She's a buzzkill."

But Georgia ignored her, hopping up from her chair and wrapping her arms around Kline's neck. She kissed him firmly on the mouth before asking, "What are you doing here, baby?"

He grinned down at her and slid a piece of her now dark locks behind her ear. "I heard the whole gang was in Phoenix. I didn't want to miss out."

"Everyone but Thatcher," Cassie added, and Kline's grin grew bigger.

CHAPTER 9

Thatch

Knock knock.

Ah, fuck.

I tried to rub the sleep from my eyes as I rolled over to look at the clock on the hotel nightstand. 6:37 a.m.

Last night had been a late one. Knowing that Cassie was spending her evening out to dinner with not only Georgia, but also Wes and Winnie, I'd used the time to catch up on all the work I'd been missing while following my pregnant fiancée around in a city that should've been known for its sweltering heat instead of its desert landscapes and mostly sunny days. It was safe to say I was ready for this weekend to be over.

Much to Cassie's dismay, last night I had chosen work over our nightly Skype session. But it wouldn't do me all that much good, following her around on some misguided journey of paranoia, only to let my company crumble to the ground so she had to take my kid and leave me because I lost all of our money and couldn't support them.

Just what I needed. Another doomsday scenario.

Knock. Knock. Knock. Knock.

Fucking hell, I was going to kill someone.

"I'm coming!" I called out blindly to the door as I rolled out of the bed and forced my upper body straight up and my legs to stand.

Knock. Knock. Knock. Knock.

Face like thunder, I charged for the door and yanked it open to nothing. No person demonizing my sleep, no maid asking to clean my room on Portuguese time, and no circus animals. But as I looked down to my feet to stave off an ounce of my anger so that it wouldn't boil over, I saw that there was a plain, brown paper package on the floor. *Open Me* was written in permanent marker on the top.

Resisting the urge to follow my own, very different instructions, of *Smash Me into a Million Fucking Pieces*, I picked up the package, slammed my door, and dropped it onto the table five steps inside the entryway to my room.

BeepBeep, the package squawked.

I'm not ashamed to admit I jumped back a step.
Okay, maybe I'm a little ashamed, but you would've jumped, too.

BeepBeep, it sounded again. "Come in, Thatch. Over."

What the fucking fuck?

That was Georgia's voice.

Carefully, like it was a goddamn bomb, I unwrapped the corners one at a time, slid the plain white box out from the paper, and opened it slowly. A lone walkie-talkie sat tauntingly inside.

"Thatcher Kelly, come in," Georgia said, her most serious voice mocking me with each word.

I snatched it from the box, keyed the mic, and put the stupid thing to my lips.

"What the fuck is going on here, Georgia? And, yes, I can tell it's you. Is Cassie with you?"

If she was, I was so fucked.

The silence went on too long, to the point that I got frustrated. "Answer me, goddammit."

"You have to say 'over' so I know it's my turn to talk. Over."

"My patience is really fucking thin right now." I paused for a second before squeezing my eyes tight and cursing to myself. "Over."

She giggled.

"Goddammit, Georgia. I'm seriously five seconds from wringing your pretty little neck—"

"Watch yourself, you fucking prick," Kline interrupted.

"*Kline?*" I asked. Jesus. What, were they all there mocking me?

"Yep," Kline answered stonily thanks to my empty threat. He and I both knew I'd never manhandle Georgia in a way that could bring her harm. But fuck, I guess neither of us thought I'd turn into a stalker either.

Apparently unaware they had the mic still keyed, Georgia and Kline's conversation played out into the otherwise silent air of my room.

"Kline! You have to say 'over.'"

"I'm not saying 'over,'" he told her, a smile evident in the lilt of his voice.

"Baby! You have to say it. That's the only way Thatch knows it's his turn to talk."

"Where did you learn this shit?" Kline asked. But I could tell he was just barely holding back laughter.

"You know I was watching *Dog the Bounty Hunter* the other day—"

"Guys!" I interrupted on a shout, a shrill squeal ringing out at the moment my walkie-talkie tried to overpower theirs.

"Can someone tell me what the hell is going on?"

"Come to your door," Kline instructed.

Georgia couldn't help herself, adding, "Over."

I shook my head but charged back to the door nonetheless. Bonnie and Clyde were rounding the corner, twisted up in each other, smiles on their faces. I stepped outside, propping the door open with one big foot.

"What are you doing here?" I asked, and Kline knew I was addressing him directly.

His face was pseudo-serious as he directed, "Let's talk inside. We don't want to wake anyone up."

"Oh, yeah," I agreed on an unmistakable growl. "We wouldn't want that."

They sure hadn't been worried about waking me up.

Kline raised his eyebrows, and knowing the son of a bitch could outwait me on nearly any fucking thing, I sighed deeply, pushed the door open, and waved for them to precede me.

Georgia smiled big and patted me on the face like a grandmother as she walked past, and Kline's amusement couldn't have gone unnoticed if I'd been in space.

As soon as the door shut, I took their walkie-talkie and tossed it across the room, so it bounced on the bed with a thump. Both sets of their eyes followed and then swung back to me, but their smiles never left their cute little faces.

"This is the most ridiculous thing you've ever been a part of," I told Kline.

"And yet, I still look sane compared to you."

They knew what I was doing. That much was clear. Now I just needed to figure out what the hell they intended to do about it.

"Don't get too excited. That doesn't mean much these days." I scrubbed my hands up and down my face and then admitted with a hefty load of self-deprecation, "I'm stalking her, for fuck's sake."

"We know," Georgia agreed with glee. "It's fantastic."

Two very separate, but equally important issues to be addressed, all in one little statement.

"How do you know?"

Kline tilted his head, and I sighed. Give him enough time, and he'll figure motherfucking anything out.

"Okay. Fine. Next issue. Why the fuck do you think it's fantastic? You want my baby to have an insane father?"

"It's just so sweet," Georgia swooned, and my eyebrows drew together.

Kline laughed and added, "In a totally fucked-up, illegal, mentally ill kind of way."

Georgia sighed dreamily. "Yeah."

"So, what? What now? Are you going to tell Cassie?" I looked right into Georgia's eyes.

"Nope."

"No?"

"I said 'nope,'" she repeated, starting to get exasperated.

"Okay. Why not? I thought you'd be running to rat me out. Isn't that what women do?"

"Easy, Killer," Kline warned as Georgia's face transformed with female affront.

Shit.

"Sorry. Sorry. Jesus. I just don't understand. What's with the walkie-talkie? Why didn't you just knock on my door and tell me to my face."

"Because we're going to help you."

"You're going to help me...*stalk* Cassie?"

Where was the *Twilight Zone* music? Seriously. It had to start soon.

Kline shrugged, but then clarified, "We're not really going to help as much as we're going to watch. And fuck, when Georgia suggested the walkie-talkie bit, I couldn't deny it was brilliant."

"Why?" I nearly yelled. I didn't understand. I didn't even understand my own drive to be involved in something as ridiculous as this, but I really didn't understand Kline's. He was Mr. Practicality. Mr. Rational. Mr. I-Don't-Do-Stupid-Shit-Like-All-of-My-Friends-Do.

"It's entertaining."

Georgia nodded enthusiastically. "Really entertaining."

I closed my eyes, tipped up my head to the ceiling, and pressed my hands desperately into my face. "Fuck me. Seriously, Kline?"

"Definitely." He gestured to Georgia. "We're happy, and you know, sane, so we don't do any of this shit on our own—"

"Thanks so much," I muttered.

"But you guys are still really finding your way, and quite frankly, it spices things up for us."

"My psychosis is your goddamn kink?"

Georgia laughed outright, clasped her hands together, and nearly jumped up and down.

"Don't worry," Kline said as he ushered Georgia toward the door. "It'll be over before you know it, and then we'll use Wes and Winnie for our entertainment. It's brewing. I can feel it."

I wanted to scream and yell and carry on, but at the same time, I couldn't deny my fucking palpable desire to be on their side of things. To watch Wes and Winnie suffer through torment and torture as I laughed maniacally on the sidelines.

God-fucking-dammit.

Kline winked just before the door closed behind him.

CHAPTER 10

Cassie

"Perfect, Quinn. Just a few more like this, and I think we can move on to the workout photos."

My camera shuttered in quick succession as I continued to take photos of the Mavericks' quarterback posing in nothing but his football pants. We had scouted out a really cool location in Phoenix for the pictorial Georgia's marketing team had hired me to shoot. And I had a moment of silent satisfaction when the urban landscape of red-brick buildings and darkened alleys managed to highlight the strong and lean lines of the rookie quarterback the exact way I had visualized when searching for this setting.

"Front cover material, Cass?" Quinn asked with a cocky grin.

I laughed. "Now you know I can't play favorites, Q. It will make all the other boys jealous."

He grinned and flashed a wink in my direction, but it failed to hold the power of Thatch's signature move.

God, I missed that man. Normally, I'd be half sated from late-night Skype sex with my favorite penis, but our nightly ritual whenever I was out of town hadn't happened before I fell asleep.

Something was up with Thatcher.

I didn't know what, but I knew when he texted me and said the Wi-Fi in our apartment was fucked up, he was definitely hiding something. Call me Crazy, but I knew the Supercock wouldn't have let anything stand in the way of screen time with my tits.

"I think we're all set here," I said as I stood up from my kneeling position. "Quinn, go on ahead into the makeup tent and get changed for the team workout photos. We need to head over to the next location in about fifteen minutes to stay on schedule."

My phone buzzed in my back pocket, and I looked at the screen to find a text from T.

> *Thatch: I'm seeing a lot of charges on my credit card from last night…*
> *Me: Maybe you should learn to never cancel Skype sex.*
> *Thatch: How on Earth did you spend $2000 on Amazon?*
> *Me: Books.*
> *Thatch: Books? You planning on opening your own library?*
> *Me: I'm planning on replacing sex with reading.*
> *Thatch: Take it back. Your tits would never speak such blasphemy.*
> *Me: They're mad at you.*
> *Thatch: I'll make it up to them. Tell them I love them and I miss them and I'll suck on their perfect pink nipples for hours when you get home.*
> *Me: Not interested.*

Obviously, I was. Hell, my nipples were already hard at the thought. But Thatch needed to grovel for a good while before I'd admit to that.

Thatch: Don't be mad, honey. I'm sorry I canceled Skype sex.
I swear I'll never do it again.
Me: Peddle your bullshit promises to someone who cares.

I watched the text bubbles move as he typed out a response.

Thatch: My hand is a piss-poor substitute for your perfect
pussy.

Before I could even think of responding, he quick-fired two
more.

Thatch: I didn't even jerk off last night. I couldn't. Nothing
feels as good as you do, honey. I'm so fucking hard for you.
God, Cass, I miss you so much.
Thatch: You still there?
Me: Keep going…
Thatch: I love you, Crazy. I love you and that most likely
crazy but beautiful baby girl growing inside your belly. Come
home, honey. I miss my family.
Thatch: Phil misses you too. He's been moping around since
you left.

Poor Phil. The mere thought of him sad and mopey had me
two seconds away from bursting into tears. Stupid pregnancy hormones.

Me: Even though you were an asshole last night, I miss you
too, T. So much. Call me so I can talk to Phil.
Thatch: I'm actually not at home right now, baby. I'm getting
ready to meet a client for a late lunch at Alberto's.

My brow furrowed as I read through the message. Thatch going into the tattoo shop on a Saturday seemed legit, but a client meeting? On the weekend? It would've been more likely to see Phil grow wings and fly around our apartment.

Me: On a Saturday?
Thatch: Unfortunately, yes.

Like I said, something was up.

Me: But you never do meetings on Saturday.
Thatch: What's the point of being at home on a Saturday when you're not there?
Thatch: Answer: There is no point.

Evasive response laced with charm. Thatch was undoubtedly up to something, and I was undoubtedly going to figure it the fu-fluff out.

Me: Gotta go. Getting ready to start shooting again.
Thatch: Love you, Crazy.
Me: I know ;)

I searched Alberto's NYC and found their number quickly thanks to Google. The line rang three times before someone picked up. "Alberto's. How may I help you?" a man with a strong Italian accent greeted.

"Hi, I'm supposed to meet a man named Thatcher Kelly for a late lunch this afternoon, and I'm running a few minutes behind schedule. What time is his reservation?"

"I have no reservation for Mr. Kelly this afternoon, *signorina*."

My lips pursed together in irritation. "Are you sure?"

"Yes, I'm sure. I know Mr. Kelly very well, and he has no reservation for today. Has there been a mix-up?"

"Oh, you know what? Maybe I got the restaurant confused. I'll just call him directly. Thanks for your help," I said and ended the call.

That sneaky son of a butter knife had lied to me!

He *lied*. To *me*.

I stared at the cracks in the red-brick wall across from me as I searched my brain for answers. Why would he lie? What in the hell was he hiding from me? Nothing made sense, but there was one thing I was certain of—Thatcher Kelly was in big flipping trouble.

Before I read him the riot act, I knew there was one person who probably knew what was up, which meant my best friend, Georgia, who also happened to be a terrible liar, would know too.

First order of business, finish up the last part of this shoot.

Second, find Kleorgie and trick them into telling me what was going on.

Third, Google cruel and unusual punishments.

Then, it was game on, motherfluffer.

CHAPTER 11

Thatch

Standing in a darkened corner of a sports facility five miles outside of Phoenix, with eyes on the love of my life, I watched as she got down on the ground and took several pictures—from between the legs of the Mavericks' star running back.

It was almost surreal, watching her lie between another man's legs, knowing she was looking for the best lighting and angle to enhance the appearance of his dick in his uniform pants and not being upset about it.

But I wasn't.

Pride surged through my veins as she worked, knowing she'd built this career and her reputation for herself. She'd put in the hours and the effort, just like I had with everything I did. And now that she was pregnant, society expected her to make a fucking choice—everything she'd worked toward or everything she'd always longed for personally. There was an illusion that she could have both, but something would suffer. *Something* would have to give.

And she was working so hard now, traveling so much, not resting at all, so that the thing that took a back seat *wouldn't be* me and our kid.

A little sacrifice now for a big reward later.

It really hadn't hit me until now, but she awed me.

And I'd done what I had to do. But now I had to stop. I had to trust her to look out for herself and our baby because, really, she already was.

She was giving everything to it.

Resting my back on the wall, I pulled myself around the corner and took a breath—and saw a shadowy figure at the other un-well-lit end of my hiding spot.

Kline.

"Are you really following me right now?"

"Yes," he answered shamelessly and began a slow walk in my direction with his phone held in front of him, pointed straight at me.

"Are you fucking recording me right now?"

He grinned. "I promised Benny I wouldn't let her miss anything."

"Where is Georgia girl?" I asked when she didn't jump out of the shadows behind him and tackle me to the ground. "And seriously, stop fucking recording me."

"Bathroom break," he replied, completely unfazed by my irritation. Slow as molasses, he continued recording for what felt like an eternity until he finally flipped his camera off and slid his phone back into his pocket.

"Did you get enough evidence to seal my imprisonment should Cassie decide to press charges?"

He chuckled. "At least five minutes' worth of footage that should be permissible in court."

In Georgia's absence, and without the Kleorgie version of paparazzi in my face, I took the opportunity to talk to him one-on-one.

"I'm surprised at you."

"Why?" he asked calmly, his friendly face shining perfectly in the light. He was always so fucking calm. The only time I'd ever seen him truly lose his cool was when everything wasn't perfect in Kleorgie land.

"It's so far out of your normal," I explained, "you know, mature, adult decisions."

"This is adult," he insisted, and I knew immediately—he wasn't talking about himself. I thought about redirecting him, but in the end, it seemed pointless. This conversation was going to end up being about me one way or another, so I might as well get it over with.

"How the fuck do you figure that?"

"Because you're thinking about someone other than yourself. Someone whom you happen to love and care about, but also respect enough not to belittle her independence."

"Dude. I'm stalking her."

He laughed, the lines at the corners of his eyes crinkling. "Yeah, but not really." I scoffed. "Sure, she doesn't know you're following her, but guaranteed, if it wasn't an invasion of her independence or about keeping her quote-unquote 'safe,' she'd invite you along with her. You're not stalking some random woman here. She wants your company."

"Right. And that makes it healthy."

"No," he agreed with another laugh. His hands dove into the pockets of his jeans, and his head bent forward before his eyes raised back to mine. "It's definitely not healthy. But the sentiment behind it is. You're fucking outrageous, we both agree on that, but it's also seriously sweet."

"What? Does Georgia's pussy have some sort of crazy Kool-Aid? You may need to take it easy on the eating her out if this is the result."

He shook his head. "I know what you're doing, trying to distract me by mentioning Georgia's pussy so I'll get riled up and forget all about talking about you, but it's not going to happen."

"Fuck." Goddamn him for knowing me so well.

"You're simultaneously putting her before yourself and doing what you have to do to find some level of comfort. It takes a lot of self-control not to put your issues on someone else, especially when it's about something as important as the safety of your unborn child."

"Yeah, that's what I hear all the time. Stalking someone and self-control in the same breath," I muttered, but he kept talking and did it with a smile.

"Sometimes, things appear one way from the outside looking in—and completely different from the inside out. In this case, it may seem like the most childish behavior you've ever displayed, but to me, someone who really knows you, it looks like you're really and truly growing up."

Fuck, this bastard could give one hell of a speech when he wanted to. It was all I could do to stop the tears from flooding my eyes.

"She's lucky to have you. Psychotic behavior and all."

"Kline?" Georgia questioned as she stepped out at the other end of the hall.

"Down here, baby," he answered her immediately, holding out an arm to claim her before she even got within thirty feet of him.

My friend was the happiest he'd ever been in his whole goddamn life. So much so, he was getting his jollies from following me as I stalked Cassie.

Georgia got to us and peeked around the corner.

"Good God," she breathed. "She's lying right under one of the guys in a push-up position."

I smirked, but I didn't take the bait. I didn't need to look anymore.

"I think I might want to make a career change," she teased.

Kline smiled at her, his heart in his eyes, and then turned back to me with a wink and lowered his voice when he noticed the change on my face. He could sense the realization I'd just come to like an infrared sensor could sense a human being.

"My little boy is growing up."

I scratched the side of my face with my middle finger.

"And thank God for that," he went on. "Because I definitely can't lift you any longer, and I'd rather do just about anything than help you in the bathroom."

I shook my head and laughed. "Fuck off."

Georgia turned back to us with her eyebrows in her hairline. "What'd I miss?"

Both of us answered at the same time.

"Nothing."

It didn't happen often, but this moment was just between us.

"Although I love being your source of entertainment, I'm going to head out," I said and pushed off the wall. "Keep Cassie company for me."

As I walked toward the exit door, Kline's voice asked from behind me, "Where are you headed?"

"I've got some errands to run."

"But Cassie's still here," Georgia said, probably out of displeasure that she couldn't watch me act like a deranged lunatic more than anything else.

"I know," I said over my shoulder as I pushed the door open. Sunlight filtered into the darkened hallway, and I turned to face them with my back holding the door open. "She's good. Should anything happen, she's surrounded by everyone I trust. And more than that, I trust her. She's going to be the best mother to our baby—because she already is. She's doing all this for us. It's time I start realizing that."

Georgia's face turned down in disappointment. "Not gonna lie, Thatch, I was really enjoying the whole stalking bit."

I grinned, and she returned my smile. This time, her voice was soft and one hundred percent serious.

"But I'm also enjoying this side of you, too."

I winked and headed out into the parking lot, confident that my favorite woman on the planet was also the very best woman to watch out for our baby. There was something I needed to do before this outrageous weekend came to a close.

CHAPTER 12

Cassie

While everyone broke down the set and packed up our equipment, I made it a priority to find Georgia and Kline. I'd see them wandering around the shoot, hand in hand and with the biggest goddamn smiles on their faces. But it wasn't just the smiles that'd had my Spidey-senses on high alert. It was the constant glances I'd noticed Georgia take as she walked around the set. Like she had been looking for something. Like she was up to something.

Yeah, *something* was definitely the opposite of mother-fuck-fluffing down.

I slid my camera bag over my shoulder and strode toward the hallway I'd last seen Big Dick and Wheorgie strolling. As I turned the corner, I found their backs to me, hunched over a phone, too riveted by whatever they were looking at to notice me coming up behind them.

"Boo!" I shouted when I was a mere two feet from them.

Georgia squeaked in surprise while Kline remained unfazed, slyly locking his phone screen and slipping it into his back pocket.

"Jesus, Cass!" she exclaimed with a hand to her chest. "You scared the crap out of me! I nearly peed myself."

Kline just chuckled and wrapped his arm around her waist, tucking her into his side.

"What are you guys doing down here?"

Her eyes went wide for a beat before she schooled her face into neutrality. Georgia had been practicing her lying skills. "Uh… Just—"

Kline chimed in. "Georgie was looking over Leslie's Instagram."

"Oh, hel-ck yes!" I held out my hand. "Let me see! I want to see what Loose Leslie has been up to lately."

Surprisingly, Kline obliged, pulling his phone out of his pocket and unlocking the screen before opening his Instagram app.

I snuck a glance at Georgia and noted her silent panic as he handed me his phone. I looked through his Instagram searches, and sure enough, there she was, @LaLaLeslieLaLa, the most recent search in his browser.

Kline might have been smart enough to cover their devious tracks, but my ears didn't miss the sigh of relief escape from Georgia's lips.

These two knew something I didn't, and I was going to get to the bottom of it.

Right the fluffernutter now.

I pretended to scroll through Leslie's pictures, even though I already followed her account religiously. This chick's social media was better than the Kardashians hopped up on meth, posting Snapchat videos. I paused on one very ridiculous photo of Leslie with a shot glass nestled inside her cleavage. Her jet black locks had been dyed blonde, and her cliché comment of "Blonds have more fun. Winky face" sat below the picture.

Yes, she literally spells out "winky face."
If you find enjoyment out of Max Monroe telling you my and
Thatch's story, imagine what a book filled with Leslie would look
like…
Exactly my point.
Someone needs to start a petition to get that book written right the
fluff now.

"Hashtag someone got bigger implants," I added.

"That's what I said!" Georgia agreed and poked Kline in the chest. "I told you!"

He just shook his head and chuckled in response. "I refuse to add commentary on anything related to Leslie or her plastic assets."

Even though I had the urge to let my inner psycho bitch come out to play and run off with Kline's phone and lock myself in the safe confines of the bathroom so I could search for evidence, I kept it classy and handed back his phone.

Obviously, pregnancy looked good on me. Well, besides when I was ugly crying over YouTube videos of soldiers coming home to their families because yeah, *no one* can pull off the ugly cry.

"Hey, have you heard from Thatcher today?" I asked Kline in a nonchalant tone.

"No, why?" he asked while his facial expression stayed irritatingly neutral. His poker face was on point. *Goddammit.* The man could play Switzerland better than anyone I knew.

"Just wondering." I shrugged. "He's been acting weird lately. Canceled our nightly Skype sesh last night. And then couldn't chat on the phone when I had a few free minutes this afternoon."

"I know he's been taking some Saturday meetings with clients while you've been out of town," he offered, and it only added to my frustration.

Damn Kline and his crazy-smart brain. He was too flipping

intelligent to be tricked into telling me what Thatch was up to, which was why I set my sights on his wife, Mrs. I Suck at Lying.

"Don't you think that's weird, Georgie?"

She cleared her throat, which put her at about a two on the "Wheorgie's About to Break" meter. "Do I think what's weird?"

"That Thatcher canceled our Skype sesh last night."

She shrugged and kept her face impartial. "Maybe he was tired?"

I watched the line of her throat swallow three times, and I knew I had just increased her to about a five. We're getting closer...

"Hmm... Maybe." I pretended to think it over and then pushed out an Oscar-worthy sigh from my lungs. "I just have this awful feeling I can't shake. It's freaking me out a little. Like, this nagging feeling that has my brain racing with thoughts that Thatch is up to something." I looked away and pretended to swallow down emotion before meeting her now concerned eyes. I forced my eyes to go theatrically wide. "You don't think he's..." I feigned shock and covered my mouth with my hand. "God, I can't even say the words," I muttered for dramatic effect.

Before she could offer the reassurance that rested on her lips, I covered my mouth with my hand and did my very best impression of Rose when Jack lets go of her hand during *Titanic*. "Sorry," I whispered and scrunched my eyes together to stave off the fake tears. I covered my mouth with my hand again and shook my head back and forth. "I just can't shake this feeling that something awful is going on."

Of course, I knew my fiancé wasn't cheating on me. That might sound naïve to most, but I knew Thatch. I knew him, and I trusted him implicitly. He'd never given me any reason to doubt that trust.

Plus, he knew that him cheating on me would lead to a homicide situation. He might be one big-ass motherfluffer, but I'd find a shovel and a hole big enough—and if I couldn't, I'd train as a blacksmith and a gravesite attendant and *make* them.

Georgia's eyes went wide with panic. "Stop thinking like that. There's no way he would… Thatch loves you. No way would he do anything to jeopardize that. You guys are in love—you're having a baby. Yeah, he's definitely not doing what you're thinking he's doing," she rambled.

And there it was, ladies and gentleman. Georgia had just hit a nine on the meter. Only a few more fake tears and she'd be handing me the key to Thatchora's box of lies.

"Yeah, but Jay Z loved Beyoncé and look what happened to them. He cheated on her. And no one thought Britney would cheat on Justin. I mean, they wore matching denim outfits, for frankfurter's sake!"

"Just trust me. He's not fucking around." She tried to calm me down, but she sounded so helpless, so upset…so very close to telling me what was going on.

I feigned hysteria and buried my face in my hands. "What am I going to do? I'm pregnant, and my fiancé is having a relationship with another woman!"

"Kline," she whispered, "I'm telling her."

"Wait. Ben—" he started to interrupt, but she was already set in her decision.

"He's here."

"—ny." Kline's shoulders sagged in defeat.

I lifted my head from my hands. "What do you mean, he's here?"

Georgia looked at Kline for a little reassurance.

He gestured toward me. "Well, fuck. No going back now, Benny."

"What was I supposed to do?" she asked with a hand on her hip.

"Realize that Cassie is a really good actress."

Georgia turned and looked at me. Her eyes interrogated my no longer distraught face. Her concerned expression turned to a glare within seconds. "How can you be so evil yet growing my sweet little baby godson inside your belly at the same time?"

I shrugged. "It's a gift."

"You're an asshole."

I covered my belly with both hands. "Hey, watch your fluffing language. My kid can hear you."

She just stared back at me and then shouted toward my stomach. "Your mother is an asshole!"

That made me laugh, and Georgia flipped me off…with both hands.

"All right, just go ahead and spill it, G. Why is Thatch here? And if he's here, where in the heck is he?"

"I'm not telling you anything else."

"Oh, c'mon. Don't be like that."

She shook her head and, surprisingly, stood her ground. "Nope. Not happening. Figure it out on your own."

I looked between her and Kline a few times before realizing I knew plenty of ways to figure out what was going on. Thatch might be a world-class prankster, but I knew all of his cards. Every. Single. One.

"Oh, don't worry, sweet cheeks, I will." I winked and turned in the other direction. As I strode back down the hallway, I called over my shoulder, "But, hey, thanks for the info, Wheorgie! You're a sweetheart for telling me he's here."

"Asshole! You're ruining all of my fun," she shouted back, and I just grinned in response.

So, Thatch was here, and whatever he was doing, Kline and Georgia were getting amusement out of it. Yeah, I'd crack this case wide fluffing open.

I was back at our hotel fifteen minutes later and standing

in front of the bellhop, ready to start Plan A of my "Where is Thatch-o?" situation.

"Excuse me," I politely asked the twenty-something man behind the desk. "I was wondering if I could find out someone's room number. I completely forgot the number he told me, and I'm already a few minutes late in meeting up with him."

"Of course. What's his name?" the man asked with a smile as he tapped the mouse of his computer, bringing it back to life.

This is why it's a good idea to go sans bra. No way this shithead would have given me this information without a hint of my nipples in play.

I knew if Thatch was on some covert mission, he wouldn't use his actual name to reserve the room. So, I went with my very best guess. His idea of the perfect porn name should he ever decide to join the sex industry. "Phil Latio."

His green eyes went wide as saucers. *"Fellatio?"*

"No." I shook my head and bit back my grin. *"Phil,* P-h-i-l. *Latio,* L-a-t-i-o."

"Oh." His cheeks flushed the color of a cherry-flavored Charms Blow Pop. *"Phil Latio."*

In my scheming, slightly evil but very hilarious brain, this conversation had now become a challenge for how many times I could get this guy to make everyone in the lobby believe he was talking about actual fellatio.

"I'm surprised you haven't heard of him."

"Phil Latio?"

There's three.

"Yeah, he's actually pretty famous."

"Mr. Phil Latio is famous?"

Four.

"Oh, yeah," I lied. "He's a very popular porn star."

He offered an amused grin. "I guess the name makes sense now."

I smirked and nodded my head.

His eyes searched my face in question, and I knew what he was asking before he found the strength to will the words out of his mouth. He was damn near gagging over the curiosity of whether I was a porn star, too.

"I'm actually writing his tell-all book," I continued the lie. "It's really a shame he had to make such an abrupt departure from the porn industry, with the whole penis transplant fiasco." I feigned sympathy. "He had the best money shot in the business."

"Penis transplant?" he blurted out.

"Yep," I answered as I tapped my fingers across the marble of the hotel desk. "It's all very new-age. He'll be one of the first penis transplants in the world. Fingers crossed it all goes well, right?"

I could tell it took all of his strength to force his face into something other than complete and utter shock laced with, "I'm going to tell everyone I work with about Mr. Phil Latio and his bionic penis."

"Yeah," he said, clearing his throat a few times. "I really hope it goes well for him."

"Did you happen to find his room number?"

"Oh, right," he muttered. "Give me just a second here." He clicked the mouse a few times and scrolled the screen until he nodded. "Mr. Phil Latio is in room 455."

And there's five.

I grinned like the Cheshire cat. "Thank you so much. Have a fantastic rest of your day."

There were going to be some seriously uncomfortable looks in my baby daddy's future.

Serves you right for lying to me, T.

As I hopped on the elevator and headed toward my room to strategize my second move, I couldn't deny that I felt elated and giddy and was practically bouncing around on the balls of my feet from the excitement.

I hadn't felt this surge of adrenaline since the early stages of our prank war.

I was hit with a wave of sentimental emotion.

This feels like the good old days all over again, before Thatcher finally realized I'm the ultimate prankster.

Get ready, Phil Latio. I'm coming for you, and it won't be for the money shot.

Okay, yeah, maybe it would be, but *after* I wrung his neck.

CHAPTER 13

Thatch

With the too hot Arizona sun shining directly in my eyes and the birds chirping their delight, I lifted my face to the sky and breathed in the possibilities of what I was cooking up. I knew no woman could resist a man who was truly in love with her, his intentions as pure as the driven snow, even when he was being a world-class idiot. Because, really, if they could, no woman would ever settle with any man. Because sometimes—oftentimes—we were idiots.

What do you expect? We're biologically driven toward sex and connection and procreation. Women were gifted with the ability to think outside the box. And I'm okay with that. I'd rather be the lesser person in our relationship. Because I know, with how hard I'm trying, that makes her one hell of a woman.

My phone rang loudly, echoing against the two-story building and drawing the attention of several women, children, and a couple of men.

I was shopping, so the numbers were slightly skewed.

This time, when I saw the name on my phone, I actually smiled.

"Hell—" I started to answer before Kline interrupted me.

"Where are you?"

Glancing around the busy Phoenix outdoor mall, I made note of all the places that would make a good hiding spot. The fountain. The children's rides. The dark hallway with the bathrooms. They had to be there somewhere.

I clucked teasingly into the mouthpiece of my phone and laughed. "I'm pretty sure you guys already know."

"Nope," he disagreed. "We stopped following you after you left the shoot. But I've got some news for you."

Instantly on alert, my smile turned upside down, and I focused on the call as hard as I could. "Good or bad? Is Cassie okay?"

"Oh, yeah, she's fine."

I took a deep breath and admitted to myself, *Okay, maybe you're not* completely *over the whole overprotective thing.*

"But if you're in your room, I'd find a way to be somewhere else, and fast. Georgie let it slip that you're here—"

Let it slip, my ass. Shit.

"And knowing what I know of Cassie—"

Oh, yeah. And he didn't even know half of the truth when it came to my crazy woman.

"She's already talked the hotel into disclosing my room number," I finished for him. "Fuck."

I'd used a code name, but God knew, Cassie was deeper inside my head than anyone. She'd probably thought of that goddamn name before she'd remembered my real one. She was a prank specialist, for fuck's sake, and with the pregnancy hormones running rampant in her lithe little body, her ability was probably enhanced. That's how the fucking things worked with everything else—hair, nails…sexual appetite.

I was so fucked.

"Yep. Obviously, maybe this is a good thing," Kline went on. "You decided to stop following her anyway, so now you can enjoy the game with her tomorrow without any secrets between you."

Yeah, great. Except I'd just spent the last two hours arranging more secrets. Lots of them. Ones I still wanted to be able to conceal until the most opportune moment.

"But, since you didn't get to break the news on your own…"

Georgia squeaked with indignation in the background. "She tricked me! She's a fucking asshole!" There was some scraping and scrapping, like maybe she was grabbing at Kline's hands or the phone or tackling him to the ground or all of the above. Directly into the phone, she yelled, "Your fiancée is an asshole!"

Kline did his best to talk over her like she wasn't shrieking. "I wanted you to have a heads-up." If he had been tackled, he was doing a good job of making it sound like he hadn't been. Only Georgia and I were out of breath and hyperventilating.

He never failed to be cool as a motherfucking cucumber in all situations.

"Thanks." Advanced warning was better than nothing.

I looked down at the bags in my hands briefly before it really hit me. If I had any hope at all of pulling everything off, I was going to need help.

"Actually, I have one more favor to ask of you guys."

"Okay," Kline agreed easily with a smile in his voice. "Anything shy of grand larceny or murder, and we're probably willing."

Georgia's giggle cut right through the phone line and seemed to fill the open air around me. It was infectious, seeping in through my skin until I couldn't hold back my smile. "No murder today. Maybe next week."

Even Kline laughed at that.

"I just need you to store some stuff."

"Stuff?"

"Not drugs. Or prostitutes. Or guns."

"Oh, well, okay. As long as it's not those three things."

"Great." Glancing down at my watch, I noted the time. "Georgia?"

"Yeah?" she asked, her voice getting louder as though Kline had put her on speakerphone.

"I'm gonna need you to use some of your new skills to keep an eye on Cassie. Over."

"Don't worry, Thatch," she assured me seriously. "Her ass won't touch grass without me knowing about it. Over."

"Over and motherfucking out," I agreed as I clicked the screen to end the call.

Five tasks down. Approximately twenty to go.

Cassie

A few hours later, after I'd showered and changed out of my sweaty clothes from the shoot, I was ready to head down to Mr. Phil Latio's room and confront that clocksucker head on.

Of course, I'd also managed to shave, exfoliate, apply Thatch's favorite shade of lipstick, and toss on the tightest shirt I could find that didn't reveal a nipple. Well, it showed nipples, but that probably had more to do with the fact that I wasn't wearing a bra, and it wasn't like you could distinguish areola color.

Yeah, yeah, I know I should be mad at him right now, but I'm

looking at the big picture.
Fights always equal makeup sex. And let's be real, my puss-ay
barely let me cover her up with a skirt and panties for this occasion.

Even though I was peeved over the lying, I didn't believe
Thatch's motivation for deceiving me was malicious. Sure, I'd had
a few irrational, crazy scenarios cross my mind, but deep down, I
knew that's all they were: crazy and irrational. The man brought
me midnight snacks in bed and made my coffee every morning
for fluff's sake. He all but worshipped the ground I walked on and
never failed to show me he was devoted—one hundred percent
committed to me, this relationship, and our family.

Three quick glances in the mirror and one elevator ride later, I
stood in front of his hotel room. The numbers 455 were displayed
proudly on the door, and I rapped my knuckles a few times against
the wood.

I covered the peephole and pressed my ear against the door as
I listened for his movements inside the room, but besides the buzz-
ing of an air conditioner kicking on, I heard nothing but silence.

After three more quick knocks, I disguised my voice in a high-
pitched tone and announced, "Housekeeping for Mr. Phil Latio."

Still, nothing.

"Housekeeping for Phil Latio," I announced again as a man
holding an ice bucket walked past me. His eyes all but bugged out
of his head as my words registered.

I had to fight my laughter when I realized how ridiculous I
sounded, propositioning my cleaning services for oral. Of course,
I had to give it another go for comedic effect.

"Towels for Phil Latio? What about pillow mints? Pillow mints
for Phil Latio?"

To my satisfaction, I watched the man stop at the room four
doors down and fumble with his keycard while cubes of ice fell to

the floor. It took him a good ten times before he got the swipe motion right and gained access to his room.

I knocked on the door one last time until I called it quits and headed back into my room. My search to find Thatch and wring his neck would be continued…*after* I grabbed a bag of M&M'S from the vending machine, laid my tired ass on my bed, and watched a few episodes of *Teen Mom*.

Once I reached my room with my vending machine loot, I slipped off my heels, took off my skirt, and plopped my ass onto the bed.

I'd find him eventually, and I figured text messages were basically the same thing as sending out a search party.

I shot him a quick, neutral text **How's your day?** and flipped on the television. I only managed to down half a bag of Doritos before he responded.

> *Thatch: Terrible. I miss you.*
> *Me: Are you home?*
> *Thatch: Yes.*

"Lying popsucker motherfudger," I muttered to myself as I typed out a response.

> *Me: Since you're home, do you want to Skype? I'm all naked and cozy in bed…*

Yeah, I wasn't naked, but he didn't know that. I could undress with the speed of an Olympian if I had to.

Nine times out of ten, if I told Thatch I wanted phone sex and I was naked, I was. But the other one percent of the time, I offered without any intention of following through, just to earn some points, while painting my nails and reading through a *People* magazine.

Of course, that one percent had changed since pregnancy upped my randy scale to frightening—*or awesome*—levels. But before I got knocked up, I'd talk him into doing it old school, without the video chat element. That way, when one of our phone-sex sessions ended on day one of shark week, I could lie in bed, sporting a pair of granny panties, with an ice pack on my vagina, faking moans and doing my best to dirty-talk Thatch to completion.

But like I said, he didn't know that, nor did he ever need to know that.

> *Thatch: I think I'll pass on the Skype sex tonight, honey.*
> *Me: For the second night in a row?*
> *Thatch: Yes, but I have good reason so you can't be mad about it.*
> *Me: Unless you've come down with an incurable disease that requires a dick transplant and you're literally in the hospital waiting on your donor penis, there is absolutely no reason good enough to cancel on me and my tits two nights in a row.*
> *Thatch: Are you sure about that?*
> *Me: Yes.*
> *Thatch: Sure enough to bet on it?*
> *Me: Yes, but I'm not taking your stupid bets tonight.*
> *Thatch: But the last bet ended so well for you... Don't you remember?*
> *Me: Of course I remember.*
> *Thatch: Wait... Which bet are you thinking of?*
> *Me: The night you bet me one hour of oral and a pair of my now favorite Louboutins that I couldn't suck you off in under a minute.*
> *Thatch: So, oral trumps our first engagement?*

Whoops. But in my defense, it was the best goddamn oral effort of my life, and my red suede Louboutins were so fluffing pretty.

Me: I guess you need to up your engagement game.
Thatch: Up my game? I'm pretty sure I can't up my game if we're already engaged to be married, honey. Three times, in fact.
Me: Are you sure about that? If my memory serves me right, the last proposal was from ME, and YOU gave me a goddamn MAYBE.
Thatch: You wanna marry me?
Me: I'll have to think about that later. I'm too busy staving off insanity because I'm all horned up and you don't wanna bone me via Skype.
Thatch: Can I bone you in person?

Three knocks to my door followed his message.

Thatch: Open the door, honey.

Slowly and without urgency, I got out of bed and walked toward the door. I opened it on a swing and came face-to-face with Thatcher, standing in my doorway, looking so goddamn good in jeans and the "Cassie's Bitch" T-shirt I'd bought him months ago that I swore Zeus himself had sent me my very own version of a Greek god straight from Mount Olympus.

"You're not at home."

"You're not naked."

We both blurted out in accusation, and the big, bad, lying man had the audacity to look upset over my tiny white lie. I poked him directly in the chest on a hard jab. "Don't try to turn the tables on me, *Phil Latio*. I know you've been lying like a mothertrucker all weekend."

"Are you going to invite me in so I can explain?"

I shrugged. "I don't know… Should I?"

He nodded and had the nerve to flash his version of puppy-dog eyes. I hated when he did that. If I had a nickel for how many times he ended up getting a blow job from that look alone… Well, I'd have a lot of fudging nickels.

I acquiesced and held the door open but kept my expression neutral, even though I had the overwhelming urge to throw myself into his arms and breathe him in. When my nose caught a whiff of his body wash and cologne as he walked past me and into the room, I had to practically shove my puss-ay back inside my underwear.

Jesus. Thirsty much, you randy bitch?

Thatch sat down on the edge of the bed and said, "Come here, honey," motioning with a wave to match his words. I rolled my eyes but followed nonetheless. The sad truth was I had missed him too much not to.

He pulled me between his thighs and rested his hands on my hips as he moved the bottom of my sleep shirt up with his nose and pressed his mouth to my belly. He stayed like that for a long moment, his lips touching the skin below my belly button, and I watched as relief and happiness and overwhelming love consumed his face.

When his warm gaze met my eyes, I had to swallow a dreamy, content sigh.

He smiled. "I know it's only been two days, but God, I missed you."

"I would've thought you were too busy coming up with lies to find the brainpower to actually miss me."

He shook his head. "It wasn't like that."

"Then, what was it like? Because, honestly, even though I

know you wouldn't do anything to jeopardize what we have, I can't deny I've had a few awful thoughts cross my mind."

But who wouldn't? Being lied to wasn't one of those things that encouraged confidence and contentment. If anything, it did the complete opposite and left you feeling vulnerable and uncertain.

"I'm a little afraid to tell you the truth."

I scrunched my eyebrows together. "Well, now I'm a little afraid for the truth too."

"Cass, honey, I love you. This isn't about anything besides that, so put those outrageous thoughts out of your mind."

"Give me a reason to put them out of my mind."

A nervous smile crested his lips. "You're going to think I'm insane when I tell you this."

I quirked a brow. "What's new?"

"I've been following you," he blurted out, and I blinked. "I've been following you around because I just can't *not* know that you and our baby are okay. I'm literally driving myself crazy over the idea that something could happen to you both, and I'd never forgive myself if I wasn't there. So, yeah, I've been following you like a creepy bastard." He looked down and muttered to himself, but I couldn't make out the words. Something about jaywalking, maybe.

"So, you followed me to Phoenix to make sure we're okay?"

He nodded. Grimaced a little.

"And Seattle…and San Diego…and well, pretty much every single place you've traveled to since we found out you're pregnant."

My jaw dropped in surprise. "You've been stalking me?"

"I know," he said and gripped my hips tighter as if he was afraid I would jet out of the room. "I've reached psychopath levels of crazy here, but I couldn't stop myself. I didn't want to suffocate you with my neuroses, so I just kind of took it upon myself to keep an eye on you guys from the sidelines without standing in your way."

"You've been *stalking* me this whole time?"

"Yes." He buried his face in my stomach. "Don't leave me. I promise I'll get this under control. I swear to God, this is the last trip I'll take."

I lifted up his chin with my fingers until his gaze met mine. "You are a fluffing idiot."

"I know," he agreed, looking almost despondent—it didn't look at all right on his face.

"That is by far the sweetest thing anyone has ever done for me."

His eyes went wide in surprise. "You're not mad?"

I shook my head, and a few tears escaped from my eyes and slipped down my cheeks. He loved me so much he was losing his mind.

God, this was the best thing I'd ever heard.

"I'm the complete opposite of mad. I feel like I just fell in love with you all over again."

I pushed him down onto the bed and straddled his hips and didn't waste another second, crashing my lips to his. I kissed him hard and deep and poured everything I had into that kiss. This man, *my* man, had been stalking me for nearly two months, and hell if it wasn't the sweetest thing anyone had ever done for me.

"Fuck, Cass." He groaned against my lips as his big hands slid down my waist and grabbed my ass, pulling my hips toward his. His dick felt like it could hammer nails, and in my mind, I was already plotting out how I could melt myself down and fashion myself into the shape of one. It might be weird, but at least I'd be skinny.

As I kissed him, I whispered against his lips, "I have something to confess, too."

"Something? What something?" he asked, slightly distracted by testing the weight of my tits in each hand like an actual scale.

"I lied to the bellhop when I asked him for your room number," I admitted as I licked across his jaw. He groaned and leaned forward, nuzzling my breasts like pillows. Or maybe he thought he could make the fabric of my shirt disappear by scrubbing it off with his face. "I think he might think you're a famous porn star who had to quit the industry because you're waiting on a penis transplant."

He leaned back and stared up at me. "He *might* think that?"

I shrugged. "Okay, so he definitely thinks that."

"And *why* does he think that?"

I scoffed. "Hello? How do you think? I fluffing told him."

"Now it all makes sense." He chuckled softly and shook his head in amusement. "Everyone behind the desk was trying to stare at my dick, you know, inconspicuously, but I just figured I had some VPL going." I raised my eyebrows and he explained. "Visible Penis Line. I saw it on one of your book blogs."

He pressed a smacking kiss to my lips and gave my ass a good, hard smack. "I should have known the stares were more intense than normal."

"Thanks to my evil ways," I declared with a laugh.

"Exactly." He shook his head and laughed again. "God, I love you."

I gazed into his smirking brown eyes and knew with absolute certainty he wasn't alone. I fell deeper under his spell a little more each day. "Is it time for makeup sex now?"

"No, honey, it's time for *marathon* sex."

He flipped me onto my back and lifted my shirt up and over my head. His fingers were sliding into my panties, and he had sucked a hardened nipple into his hot mouth before I could offer a response.

I moaned when his thumb joined the party and started rubbing smooth circles around my clit.

"Yeah, definitely marathon sex," he agreed with his earlier

comment. "I'm going to fuck you until you can't walk tomorrow."

"What about the game?" I asked, but in all honesty, I gave fluff all about that game. At that point, the only balls I was in the mood for were Thatch's.

"I'll fucking carry you," was the last thing he said before he tore off my panties, spread my thighs, pulled his perfect cock out of his jeans and buried himself to the hilt.

"Thatch, yes," I whimpered and lifted my arms so I could grip the headboard with my fingers.

"That's right, honey. Hold on tight. We're going for gold in Phoenix tonight."

I couldn't stop the laugh that bubbled up and out of my chest, but Thatch stopped it for me with a carefully placed rotation of his hips.

"Oh, holy hell," I moaned as the head of his dick put pressure on the perfect spot inside of me.

"You're everything," he whispered in my ear as I tightened my thighs around his waist. One kiss, two, he touched his lips to my neck before licking a line from my collarbone to my jaw. "Watching you these last few weeks, Cass," he went on, his voice so genuine it was nearly tortured, "I could not have imagined a better version of you."

My eyes closed and my head lolled back. An opportunist, Thatch used the space to lick his way down my chest until his lips met my breast.

His hips worked faster and deeper, seeking every inch of connection he could get, and I welcomed it. Warmth and love danced in his eyes as he lifted them to meet mine, and I fell right down their well.

Into comfort and safety—and right into my orgasm.

It took me by surprise, so sudden, so powerful, but Thatch didn't look surprised at all; he looked like he'd been waiting.

Waiting for me and this moment and everything we were and would ever be.

"You're everything too," I told him softly as he groaned through the height of his climax.

And he was—everything I'd never been smart enough to hope for.

CHAPTER FOURTEEN

Wes

Winnie stood at the side of the field in casual clothes—or so she would describe them.

To me, there was nothing casual about the way her jeans framed and lifted her ass or the sight of all that perfect, creamy skin revealed by the sleeveless cut of her tank top.

It was hot as balls here, even in October, and I didn't blame her for dressing down a little. There was no reason to come to the last walk-through practice in femme-fatale battle gear, but I'd thought she was only dangerous in those skirts and crisp business shirts. In her daily gear, she was like something out of my teenage wet dreams—the ones that used to make me *actually* come in my sheets.

Yep. I'm admitting to that. Any man who doesn't is a liar.

Quinn Bailey stepped back, shuffling out of the pocket with ease and lobbing a light pass over the heads of waiting defenders at the center of the field. Bransky was late to the crossover, behind the pass, and would have been demolished during a game-day scenario of this play, so the sound of the whistle from Coach Bennett's lips was no surprise.

"Bransky!" he yelled. "Get your ass back here and run it again!"

I would have laughed if it hadn't been for the expression on Bransky's face that made it look like Bennett had just told him his favorite grandmother died. He was still young, right out of college, and his fucking people-pleasing attitude was one in a million. The kid seriously didn't know the meaning of quit, and he was going to go places because of it. Not just in the NFL, but in life. The sad truth was, so few people worked that hard anymore.

My eyes moved back to Winnie and the white turf of the sideline under her feet. Thanks to a long-standing relationship with the president of Arizona State University, we had a place to come just outside of Phoenix, in Tempe, that wasn't the opposition's territory to run through our plays last minute—to make sure they were second nature to each and every guy on the field.

Normally, I tried to stay removed—it wasn't my job to coach, no matter how bad I wanted to—so I kept to a seat up in the bleachers.

But as much as I hated to admit it, the call of Winnie was strong. I found myself wanting to go stand on the sideline just to see if I could catch a whiff of her, and *goddamn*, that was fucking dangerous.

Thankfully, the ringing of my phone put my ass—*that was a solid inch in the air*—back on my seat.

After strongly considering sending him to voicemail, I worried that maybe something was wrong with Cassie and he needed me to do something about it. And holy hell, I'd feel like an asshole if I ignored a call like that.

I pushed the green phone icon to accept, and he started talking before I could say anything in greeting.

"I need access to the field right after the game," Thatch said, and I groaned.

"Could you maybe, every once in a while, call me when you don't want something that's nearly impossible?"

"This isn't nearly impossible," he insisted, a hint of desperation in his normally playful voice.

"This isn't a home game. This isn't my stadium, in case you've forgotten. My word doesn't rule. I can't just grant you access. I have to call Hank Bastian and ask him because it's *his* stadium. *His* field. *His* access to grant."

"Great."

"Great?"

"Yeah," he responded without missing a beat. "You obviously know how to make it happen, so do that."

"It's not that simple," I told him.

"Wes. *Please.* I want to get married on the field tomorrow, after the game. I've got everything ready. Cassie's parents are coming last minute under the pretense of watching Sean play, and I'm going to make her my wife. I need access to that field. I'm begging you. Please."

"Okay," I agreed. There really wasn't any other option.

"Thank God," Thatch exhaled, his relief so thick I could feel it coating my skin and settling deep into my gut. And despite my own feelings about marriage and kids, I couldn't stop my smile.

"Text me when you have confirmation about the field, and, yeah, yeah, I know I'm a pain in your ass, but the sooner the better. I'm really counting on it, and I have a few things to do after I get it. Plus, I've got Cassie on my ass since she found out I'm here, and I have very limited time to get all of this shit done."

"You're here?" I asked, and as soon as I did, I knew it was a dumb question.

"Uh, yeah. Hence the need for the field."

The way he said it had me narrowing my eyes. "Why do I get the feeling there's way more to this than you're telling me?"

"Because there is. A whole fuck of a lot that I'm a little embarrassed to admit and in no way have time to explain right now. But, because I'm friends with people like Kline, I'm sure you'll hear the full story soon enough."

"Okay, but—"

He cut me off. "Gotta go. Text me."

Shaking my head, I pulled the phone away from my ear and got up from my seat immediately. But this time, it wasn't for a blond-headed woman who was off-fucking-limits.

Apparently, I had to talk to Hank Bastian.

Winnie

"Nice game tonight, Bailey." I high-fived Quinn, the Mavericks' quarterback, on his way back into the locker room.

"Thanks, Dr. Double U." All of the players called me different things, from Winnie the Pooh to Winslow to Dr. W., but Quinn Bailey was a sweet Southern boy with a thicker accent than most, and the way he said my name always made me laugh. He grinned and filed down the tunnel with the rest of the team.

The Mavericks had handled Phoenix with ease, pulling out another away game win with four touchdowns and one field goal to come out ahead, 31-10. If they kept playing like this, their hopes of getting into the play-offs, and earning themselves a first-round bye, were a very real possibility.

As I passed Wes, who was walking in the opposite direction and back toward the field, he grabbed my wrist and pulled us both to a stop. "Aren't you coming?" We both looked down at his hand wrapped around me in surprise, and my heart beat a little faster.

Finally meeting his eyes, I tilted my head in confusion. "Coming where?"

"Onto the field… Wait…have you talked to Georgia in the last few hours?"

I shook my head. "I left the hotel early this morning and haven't had a chance to check my phone. Is everything okay?"

"Everything's good."

"Okay…then, what's going on?"

"Just follow me and you'll see." He tugged on my wrist gently and pulled me in the opposite direction.

I didn't put up a fight and just let him lead me down the tunnel, which was uncomfortably empty as we walked side by side toward the field. *Too empty.* Only the soft footfalls from our shoes filled the quiet. I felt the urge to break the silence, and for some insane reason, found myself blurting out, "I don't stare at your ass, by the way."

He peeked out of the corner of his eye. "Yeah, you do. But it's okay. I don't mind."

I tugged my wrist—which he was still holding for some unknown reason—out of his hold and stopped dead in my tracks. "Could you stop that?"

He paused midstep and turned to face me. "Stop what, exactly?"

"Stop saying shit like that to me. This—" I motioned erratically between us with one hand "—can never happen."

"I'm aware. Believe me, I'm well aware that nothing can happen between us, Winnie," he responded and stepped closer to me. I stepped back until my back hit the cement wall of the tunnel.

"Good," I spat.

He closed the distance between us again and braced his hands on either side of my head.

"Good," he whispered harshly.

"Fine."

"Okay." His warm breath brushed my lips, and I had the overpowering sense of déjà vu. We had been here before, in a very similar position, when I invited him into my office under the pretense of looking at Mitchell's MRI.

"It won't happen," I announced weakly, and I wasn't sure if I was saying it for me or for him.

His eyes stared at my lips. "Nope. Never."

A pregnant pause filled with uncertainty and tension and want and need and the irresistible urge to give in to what my body was so desperate for took hold of me. All I could do was stare back at him, my gaze alternating between his lips, his eyes, and then repeating that maddening circuit on a loop.

My heart raced with anticipation.

Was he going to kiss me?

Was I going to kiss him?

Before I could find the answers to those questions, the sounds of Georgia and Cassie giggling filtered into the tunnel. The sudden onslaught of noise in the silence startled me, and I wasn't the only one. Wes backed away—from me, from our almost moment—moving himself to the other side of the space and scrubbing angry hands through his hair. His hazel eyes, however, refused to let go of mine.

I fought to catch my breath as Cassie and Georgia came into view in my peripheral vision. They were smiling and laughing and completely unaware of what they had just managed to stop.

Thank God.

Yeah, keep acting thankful even though you know how much

you want that surly, broody, temperamental sex-on-a-stick man.

"Hey, guys! Great fucking game today," Georgia greeted with a warm smile. The break in the spell between Wes and me felt like the snap of a rubber band.

"What are you guys up to?" I asked in a surprisingly calm voice.

Cassie smirked. "Georgia thinks she can get an autograph from that fuckhot Phoenix running back. What are you guys doing?"

"Well, I was supposed to chat with a few reporters about today's game, but your idea sounds *way more fun,*" Wes teased. He was serious so often—too often, really—but he looked at those women with genuine affection. He laughed and smiled at their jokes, and I could tell he was pleased to see them, even when he pretended to be put out. There were things about him he concealed so well, and I *refused* to let myself want to know about them.

Georgia and Cassie laughed and then proceeded to head down the tunnel. I followed their lead and made sure I kept my traitorous body a safe distance from Wes. The last thing I needed was close proximity when I'd yet to calm down the erratic pounding inside my chest. One more situation like that with him, and I feared I might end up with a permanent arrhythmia and require a pacemaker.

The second we hit open air and our feet reached the turf, we came face-to-face with Thatch, standing proudly on the field with a giant grin covering his face as Cassie walked toward him.

Their nearest and dearest stood yards away, while the words "Marry me, Cassie Phillips" flashed bright and bold on the Jumbotron.

"What in the fluff is going on, T?" she asked as she looked around the field in surprise.

His grin grew wider as he motioned for her to close the distance between her and him, and he got down on one knee at the goal line.

Stubborn as always, she held her ground and put her hands on her hips. I could feel Wes beside me, breathing and watching and waiting to see what would happen, but he didn't make a peep. None of us did as Cassie and Thatch faced off.

"Why do I have to come to you?"

Thatch looked fit to be tied, but in the good way. Instead of tied in knots, he wanted to be tied to her, stubborn indignation and all.

Climbing to his feet again, he walked to her, and just when I thought he'd stop, he scooped her up, one arm behind her knees and the other around her back as he carried her back over to the end zone and set her down again. He didn't drop to his knee this time, instead pulling their joined hands to his chest and holding them there. "I was told I needed to up my proposal game."

"Is a fourth proposal really necessary?" Kline called out, and I gasped at the unexpected interruption.

Wes's hand reached out and took hold of mine.

Thatch just smiled and pointed to the scoreboard. All of our eyes followed his direction obediently, and it wasn't a second before the Fourth Down graphic flashed and swirled on the screen.

"Thanks, Kline," Thatch yelled, and I knew then that this was all part of the plan. "I'm so glad you asked that."

Wes barked a chuckle beside me, and I couldn't stop myself from looking up at his smile. He didn't look at me, though; his eyes were on his friends.

"Sometimes," Thatch went on, "it takes four tries, to really get it right."

"We usually try to avoid fourth downs," Sean Phillips called out, and I bit my lip to contain my tears. I wasn't big on crying, but everything was so obviously exactly as it should be. These people were so meant for each other, I was overwhelmed. Wes's hand tightened around mine.

Thatch nodded again, obviously excited that everyone was doing their part. "I know. Another excellent point, Sean."

Cassie laughed, and the sound of it echoed through the space and straight on to Thatch's already smiling face.

"Fourth downs, though, they have something special, don't you think?"

He didn't wait for anyone to answer. "They're the final frontier, the last chance, the time to *make* it happen. So that's what I'm doing here."

The big screen flashed the words "Wedding Day," and that was when I knew. This was happening, right here, right now.

"I've decided that I don't want to wait another second to make you my wife."

Cassie looked around and noticed her parents, Thatch's parents, all of us—everyone who meant something to her—for the first time.

"You are the very best thing that has ever happened to me. You're my best friend, Crazy, and I want to spend the rest of my life with you because you are my life. Marry me right now."

"As in *here,* right now?"

He nodded.

"On a football field?"

He nodded again.

"Are you crazy?"

"I think you're rubbing off on me," he teased.

He didn't have to ask her again because she was nodding her head yes and then tossing her arms around his neck and hugging him tightly. She whispered something into his ear, and he leaned back to meet her eyes. "I love you too. Now," he said as he stood up with her still in his arms, "Let's go get hitched."

Thatch carried her across the field toward the small group of their smiling family and friends standing on the fifty-yard line. Wes dragged me to follow, since we hadn't even made it out of the edge of the tunnel before everything had started to go down.

As they stood, before their loved ones and the minister who was there to make it all official, I couldn't quell the surge of emotion. I was happy for her, so very happy for her, and I was finding that, deep down, I wanted to experience that kind of love. Overwhelmed, I swiped a few tears from my cheeks, and to my surprise, Wes smiled gently in my direction as he untangled his hand from mine and discreetly handed me a small handkerchief.

Who still carries a handkerchief?

"Thanks," I whispered, but his hand didn't come back.

I wished I didn't miss it.

He nodded and went back to watching the bride and groom say their vows.

I stared at him for a long moment, memorizing the soft expression on his face as he witnessed one of his best friends marry the woman of his dreams.

Maybe Wes Lancaster had a heart buried beneath that steely, unwavering exterior after all?

Maybe he wasn't as brooding and surly as I originally thought?

Maybe I wanted to peel away those layers and get to know him?

Wait. No. I didn't want that.

Yes, you do.

Fuck.

I quickly averted my eyes from him and focused on Cassie and Thatch. He was smiling down at her as she finished her vows.

"I now pro—" The minister started to announce, but she interrupted him before he could finish.

"Oh, fluff. Wait." She held a finger in the minister's direction.

"Just one more thing," she said and turned her attention back to Thatch. "I got the results back for the blood test."

She glanced at everyone in attendance and added, "Not *that* kind of blood test, you weirdos. It was a test to make sure the baby is healthy, and the baby is very healthy, but it also detected the sex." Her eyes met Thatch's again, and she smiled.

"You know what we're having?" he asked in surprise.

She nodded and, with her heart in her eyes, said, "A boy."

His eyes shone with liquid emotion. "We're having a boy?"

Cassie's expression mimicked his as a few tears spilled down her cheeks. "We're having a boy, honey."

Thatch's face morphed into the biggest smile I'd ever seen as he wrapped Cassie up in his arms and pressed his lips to hers without delay.

"I now pronounce these two husband and wife," the minister declared on a soft laugh. "You may continue kissing your bride."

Everyone in attendance clapped their hands and exclaimed their congratulations, while Thatch and Cassie stayed oblivious to the world and continued to kiss the hell out of each other.

I wondered if I'd ever have that kind of happy ending.

My hands tingled as my blood pumped faster.

I wanted it.

Traitorously, without permission, my gaze found Wes's and stayed there.

God, I want it.

The End

Love Kline, Thatch, Wes & the Girls?

Stay up to date with them and us by signing up for our newsletter:
www.authormaxmonroe.com/#!contact/c1kcz

You may live to regret much, but we promise it won't be this.

Seriously. We'll make it fun.

If you're already signed up, consider sending us a message to tell
us how much you love us. We really like that. ;)

And you really don't want to miss what's next for
the Billionaire Bad Boys.

Wes and Winnie are coming for you in *Scoring the Billionaire* on
October 25th, 2016.

Things are about to get heated. And complicated.
But by God, these two know how to bring it.
Spoiler alert: Wes's penis is in this book. Not just the tip. His
whole penis. And sometimes, his penis doesn't wear pants.

Preorder the rest of the Billionaire Bad Boys Series here::
www.authormaxmonroe.com/#!books/cnec

CONTACT INFORMATION

Follow us online:

Website: www.authormaxmonroe.com

Facebook: www.facebook.com/authormaxmonroe

Reader Group:www.facebook.com/groups/1561640154166388

Twitter: www.twitter.com/authormaxmonroe

Instagram: www.instagram.com/authormaxmonroe

Goodreads: https://goo.gl/8VUIz2

ACKNOWLEDGEMENTS

First of all, THANK YOU for reading. That goes for anyone who's bought a copy, read an ARC, helped us beta, edited, or found time in their busy schedule just to make sure we didn't do something stupid like let Cassie slap Thatch's dick completely off. Although, he probably deserved it a few times. ;) Thank you for supporting us, for talking about our books, and for just being so unbelievably loving and supportive of our characters. You've made this our MOST favorite adventure thus far.

THANK YOU to each other. And the Golden Girls. We really love the Golden Girls. Okay, yeah, we really love each other, too. We're best friends…blah blah blah…you know the drill. Monroe thanks Max. Max thanks Monroe. We do this every book, but it's just our style. We wouldn't trade each other for anything. Writing together is the most fun we've ever had and it feels impossible to go back to the days before we started this journey. So, if it's okay with you guys, we'll just keep on making you laugh via Max Monroe style books. Also, we'll keep watching the Golden Girls because Sophia is our spirit animal. Well, unless Stock Photo Guy We Want to Bone ever calls us. Then we'll totally be Blanche. ;) #Kidding #Maybe

THANK YOU, our fair Lisa. Don't ever leave us. We love you too much. And for writing us emails with the word 'wildebeests' inside.

THANK YOU, Kristin and Murphy. Thank you never feels like enough. We don't know what we'd do without you guys. (Or daily posts/pictures of Murphy's adorable baby.)

*THANK YOU, Amy, for being you. You never fail to be the one person who can always get things done. There is no doubt about it, you are the perfect agent for us. Let's keep doing this. Sound good? ☺

THANK YOU, Sommer, for never giving up on us even though we send you ten emails in the same day asking for exactly one thousand things. You make us laugh. You make us smile. And you've made our Billionaire Bad Boys look so damn good.

THANK YOU to every blogger who has read, reviewed, posted, shared, and supported us. Your enthusiasm, support, and hard work does not go unnoticed. We wish we could send you your very own Billionaire Bad Boy as thanks. We can't. We checked with UPS and they said no. Also, there's no way in hell we could find a box big enough to fit Thatch in.

THANK YOU to the ladies of Camp Love Yourself for not sending us pictures of you literally loving yourself. Well, not too many anyway. ;) And thanks for being beautiful, amazing, and hilarious enough to let us get away with saying things like you're sending us pictures of yourselves when you're not. You're the cat's meow. Well, every cat but Walter. He doesn't really meow unless your name is Georgia.

THANK YOU to our families. Thank you for all of your patience and understanding and unwavering support. We couldn't do any of this without you. You make life grand and we love you so much. P.S. We've decided to go to the Bahamas for the entire month of January. We figured you wouldn't mind at all. You probably won't even notice we're gone.

P.P.S. Kidding!

P.P.P.S. Unless, you guys are okay with that…?

All our love,
Max & Monroe

CPSIA information can be obtained
at www.ICGtesting.com
Printed in the USA
LVHW05s2335251018
594898LV00011B/364/P